TALE OF A CHINESE

by

Xiao-ming Chen

This is a work of fiction. Any resemblance of any of the characters
to persons living or dead is strictly coincidental.

FIRST EDITION

UNIVERSITY EDITIONS, Inc.
59 Oak Lane, Spring Valley
Huntington, West Virginia 25704

Cover by Joan Waites

Dedication

To my daughter, Linda

Dedication

Author's Note

The spelling of Chinese words in this book is the new system called Pinyin. I have made only a few exceptions when the word is more familiar to the reader in its old form, for example, Peking instead of Beijing.

Acknowledgments

My special thanks go to my teachers at the University of New Mexico, Professor Rudolfo Anaya and Tom Mayer, who encouraged me to write my novel; to Marguerite Krupp, who helped me to edit; to Judie and Steve Bowen, who never hesitate to help me when I need.

Part One

A Tiny Flower

1

"Li Ling," my grandma suddenly called my name one day when we both sat on the coach near the window, reading.

"What?" Her nervous tone drew my attention away from my comic book.

"We should have a talk."

"For what?"

She swallowed hard to keep her voice calm enough to let me hear what she said. "We have to send you back to Shanghai soon."

"Why?" I cried out. I was born in Shanghai, but I went to live with my grandparents in Hong Kong when I was only two. At that time, my parents were busy starting their careers. They left me at home with a baby-sitter all day long, so my grandma took me with her to Hong Kong after she had visited my parents.

"Your parents would get into trouble if you stay with us," she said.

"Why?"

"You're too young, Li Ling. It's a political stuff not even I can understand, how can you understand?"

"But I can understand, Grandma. Please tell me. Why?"

"I don't know how to explain that," my grandma said. "You know, the social system in Hong Kong is different from that on the mainland. The government on the mainland doesn't like the people who live in Hong Kong. They think we are the bourgeoisie, and they are proletarians. I don't know why they separate us; both of us are Chinese. We are brothers and sisters. But they don't like our way. Your parents often get into trouble because we live here. Recently, they keep asking us to let you return home. I know there's certainly something troubling them. I love you, Li Ling. I want you to stay; but we can't let your parents get into trouble."

I felt dumb because I couldn't accept the fact that my grandparents were going to send me away. I was too young to know the social system or what bourgeoisie and proletariat meant. I only knew that my grandparents loved me, and I wanted to stay with them. I was so confused that I felt like a dog who had lost his owner.

I'll never forget leaving my grandparents at Guangzhou Station. It was a cloudy day. The sky was gray and the buildings in the station were gray too. The train, that would take me to Shanghai, was like a giant snake waiting for me. I held my

7

grandparents' hands tightly while they talked to my mother who had come to meet us at Guangzhou. She was a stranger to me, although her face looked like grandma's. They had the same almond-shaped eyes, thin lips and straight noses. She wore a dark blue Mao tunic suit; and my grandma wore a cream colored suit and skirt. In my eyes, my grandma was more beautiful and cordial. She hugged me as hard as she could and begged my mother to take good care of me. Suddenly, I felt my nose twitch and I began to cry.

"Oh, my baby; my poor baby," my grandma cried too.

At that moment, the bell of the train rang. I began to cry loudly. I couldn't help it. I didn't want to leave my grandparents, I didn't want to return to Shanghai. For me, home was with my grandparents.

"Don't cry, my dear. We just leave you for awhile. We'll meet again soon. Grandma promises you." Grandma choked with sobs. She kissed me and her tears mixed with mine.

I can't remember how I got on the train. It seemed I was drawn by my mother and pushed by my grandpa at the same time. As the train started to move, the figures of my grandparents outside became smaller and smaller. I cried sadly and helplessly.

"Do you want something to drink?" my mother asked.

"No," I almost screamed at her. I hated her because it was she who forced me to leave my grandparents. She smiled at me and put a bottle of lemon soda on the table. "You can have it when you are thirsty," she said.

I kept crying, because I already missed my grandparents. I don't know when I stopped crying and fell asleep. When I awoke, I was fascinated immediately by the landscape outside the window: it was something I had never seen before.

I saw some oxen pulling plows on a wide field. The small brick houses looked like my toy building blocks arranged in a row beside the road. There were a lot of hills along the way, some of them green, some of them gray and some red. I had never seen red hills before. The mud was red, the rock was red, the grass on the hills seemed red, too. The color of the mud was so red that it looked like the color of blood. My mother told me it was a red soil area, so everything was red. She seemed to know a lot. Every time I asked a question, she gave me the right answer. She opened the lemon soda for me when I looked through the window, pressing my nose against the glass. The cool juice made me feel comfortable, and I began to talk with her. She told me that the green plants in the field were wheat, the trees that had long branches were willows. There were so many things to see outside. I concentrated my attention on the screen and absolutely forgot the time.

The train passed one town after another. The scene through

the window changed fast. At last the train entered a large city. There were a lot of high buildings, but none of them as fancy as the commercial buildings in Hong Kong; a lot of people who wore the Mao tunic suits; and a lot of bicycles. The station was in the center of the city. When I saw the sign on the railway platform, I knew it was Shanghai, the home of my parents.

My mother became excited as the train gradually slowed. She sat near the window and looked out eagerly.

"Look, your father is there!" When my mother touched my shoulder, I turned to see. A man was standing on the platform looking at the train. His face was brightened up when he saw us.

"Hello, my young man," he lifted me up with arms as soon as we left the train. "How are you?"

"Fine," I said.

He kissed me and his beard stabbed my face. I whimpered and tried to turn my head away.

"Oh, be brave, my young man," my father laughed. "Someday you'll have your own brush, maybe harder than mine."

"No," I said. I would be clean shaven like grandpa, I thought.

"No? Okay, your mother will like it. A face rough with beard always keeps girls away." He looked at my mother, and she laughed, too. My father was entirely different from my grandpa. Grandpa was serious in speech and manner. He was always very polite, very courteous. He never cracked jokes with me. But my father made me feel we were equals, like friends. We walked to the exit of the Shanghai Station, and my father put his arm around me.

A taxi took us to our home, an apartment in one of the high buildings on Main Street. The apartment, which consisted of two bedrooms and one sitting room, was on the third floor. My bedroom was small but sunny and comfortable, with a blue bed covered with a white sheet and a light blue blanket. The small desk set near the windows would be very important for me. The other furniture was a chair, a wardrobe and a bookshelf. The room was the same as my room in Hong Kong, but smaller.

I went to bed early in the evening. I was so tired from the long trip that I fell asleep immediately.

It was a summer day and I could see my grandma busy in the kitchen, cooking, and my grandpa sitting on an armchair in the sitting room, reading a newspaper. He wore a light blue shirt and a dark blue tie. His shirt was buttoned up. "Eat more," he said. He picked up some meat with chopsticks and put it into my bowl. "I know you love it," my grandma said; she was cooking a yellow croaker. I stood beside her, looking at the fish. The dish was smoking. I was eating. "Take your bowl with your hand,

9

Li Ling," grandpa said. He was eating a fish tail. "A well-bred child has to hold his bowl when he's eating." "You certainly like the belly, don't you?" grandma said. My bowl was full of fish. "You can't watch T.V. anymore," grandpa said. I was in my room. The bed was made. Grandma helped me take off my clothes. I was in my bed and she sat beside me, singing a song. It was a cradle-song, soft and sweet. It lingered in the air when I awoke.

I got up early because I had to go to school. My breakfast was a glass of soya-bean milk and two steaming rolls. The steaming rolls with fresh vegetable and sesame seed oil were very delicious. My mother told me when I was eating that I would spend most of my time in school since the school had a full-time program.

It was only ten minutes walking distance between our home to the school. The shops on Main Street were all closed. There were no advertisements, no artificial ornaments; the only thing showed in front of the shops were their names. The city was quiet except when some of the buses rang their bells. The buses were single-level, each had its special color. The number 20 were blue, and the number 26 were red. In front of the school, I saw a woman just a foot taller than me waiting at the entrance. She was my teacher. After my mother said goodbye to me, she led me upstairs to the classroom where about fifty desks and chairs were set.

"Boys and girls, this is our new classmate, Li Ling, who has come from Hong Kong. From now on, he will . . ." Everyone stared at me with great curiosity when the teacher was introducing me. Their penetrating stares made me believe something must be wrong. They were curious and surprised, as if they were looking at a monster. I felt so nervous that I wondered what was wrong and why they stared at me. I turned the problem over and over in my mind until the teacher put her hand on my shoulder. She motioned for me to sit on a seat in the last row. I walked to my chair mechanically.

From the adjacent seat, a girl smiled at me. She was an exquisite girl with dark bright eyes and two deep dimples. Her smile was so sweet that it made me feel much better. I thought I would like to talk to her when class was over.

As soon as the class was over, all of the students came to me and surrounded me. They looked me up and down as if I had come from another planet. Suddenly, one of the boys shouted at me and all of them looked at my shoes. "Look! He's wearing a pair of sharptoed shoes!" I would have hidden my feet if I could have, because my shoes really looked out of place among their black cloth shoes and green sneakers. I blushed. I remembered the day my grandma accompanied me to buy the shoes. I chose

10

them after I had tried on a bunch of pairs. But in my classmates'
eyes, they were ugly. The bad feeling made me want to cry.
They all laughed at me, except the girl. "Wang Ming, how dare
you laughing at our new classmate!"

Her words had such power that Wang Ming closed his mouth
at once, but he glanced at me before he left as if to say he
would get even with me later. As soon as Wang Ming left, the
others began to ask me questions. They wanted to know where I
lived and what schools I had attended. I answered the questions
one by one, and we got to know each other quickly. But I would
never forget the look Wang Ming gave me, a look that was filled
with hate.

That evening my mother came home early. She said she
would prepare a big welcome home dinner for me. She cooked a
large yellow croaker which was my favorite, with sweet and sour
sauce.

My father poured me a glass of beer. "Cheers!" He winked
at me and smiled.

"Cheers!"

His glass clinked mine. The sound made me feel so good that
I immediately proposed a toast to his health and my mother's.

"You like the belly, don't you?" my mother said. She picked
up the whole belly for me. She said that, when I was a baby, I
liked to eat the belly of fish because the belly meat was tender
and it had less bone. She told me I had been a strange baby who
liked music so much that the only way she could make me sleep
was singing the cradle-song. She sang the song while I laughed. I
told her that grandma also could sing the same song. "Oh, yes,"
she said, "I learned it from her when I was a child."

2

I got used to my new life gradually. I changed my style and wore the same tunic suits the other students wore. I quickly made friends with the girl who sat beside me, and I called her Fang-fang as her name was Zhang Fang. She was so nice that she helped me a lot. She taught me how to write the simplified Chinese characters since I had learned only the original complex form in Hong Kong. And she explained the text to me since I couldn't understand Mandarin, the official language quite well.

Sometimes, we did homework together at her house. Her father was a professor who taught Chinese literature at Shanghai University. He was a wonderful story teller who could draw us into the different scenes as if we were part of the story. So every time we saw him, I would ask him to tell us a story. But I rarely saw him. He was always locked up in his room, writing a book.

I never tried to make friends with Wang Ming, nor did he with me. I didn't know why. It seemed natural for us to be in conflict with each other. After several sharp encounters, the battle between us could no longer be avoided.

One day I was assigned to be the student-on-duty who had to clean the class-room. I swept the floor during the break. After I had swept several rows of seats, I found some torn papers on the clean floor. "Who did it?" I asked. "I cleaned that side of the floor already."

"Me," Wang Ming said provocatively and loudly. The classmates who were in the room all turned their heads towards me and looked at me. One of them was Fang-fang. "Aren't you a student-on-duty? Okay, you have to clean the classroom whenever it is dirty." He looked at me challengingly while he threw pieces of paper on the floor.

The classroom was quiet. People stared at Wang Ming with astonishment. I felt my face getting hot and I was furious. I picked up the broom and threw it at him. In all my memory, I had never fought with anybody. My grandpa always taught me to be polite and courteous, but I was so mad that I just couldn't control myself. As soon as we came to blows, I realized that I wouldn't be able to beat him. He was taller than I was, and he was as strong as a bull. I fought hard. I knew everyone in the classroom was watching us. I could feel how anxious Fang-fang was. I seized the chance when he jumped at me. I turned back suddenly and he missed me; then I hit him on his back with all my strength, made him stagger and fall to the ground. I stood over him and waited. Fang-fang was standing by me silently. When Wang Ming got up, he bowed his head and wiped his bleeding nose. He looked up at us for awhile and then walked away.

I had beaten him. But the victory made me pay a greater price than I should have paid. Since he got a bad scratch when he fell on the ground, the teacher called my father. My father was very angry when he learned that I had fought with somebody in the class. But he didn't scold me. My only punishment was to learn to play the violin. Chinese believe that music can mend a person's temperment, and my father wanted to make me gentle and quiet by having me learn the violin. I liked music, but I didn't like to play instrument myself. Now I had to learn to play whether or not I liked it.

I was forced to visit a violin teacher as soon as my father found one. I would be taught in his house every Sunday. He was an old man, nearly seventy years old, but he looked more middle-aged since he had bright eyes and rosy cheeks. His head was bald and brown, just like a potato. He taught me how to press the violin using my neck and collarbone, and how to pick up the bow using five fingers of my right hand. I daydreamed when he spoke to me. I didn't listen to what he said; I just looked at the muscles of his face moving curiously.

"Now, Li Ling, you have to play yourself," he said. He motioned for me to pick up the violin and the bow. It sent out a terrible sound when I played. It sounded like thunder as soon as the bow touched the G string, and like a scream when the bow touched the E string.

"Well, you played pretty well," the old man said to me. I was shocked. Was my playing really well? I thought he was kidding. Perhaps he wanted to get more money from my father. He told us that we had to pay him five bucks for half an hour. To my surprise, my father agreed to the price. He said that I did a good job and I would be an excellent violinist if I spent three hours a day to practice.

I was wondering whether or not I would be an excellent violinist when the door opened and a boy, who carried a violin, came in. His eyes looked blank and his insensitive expression made me believe that he didn't like to play the violin either. As soon as he noticed me, we smiled at each other and I knew we would be good friends.

"My name is Li Ling," I told him the next time when we met.

"Me, Liu Jian-guo," he said. "I hate to play violin. I love to read novels, but my father wants me to be a violinist since he couldn't be one." He was an interesting person, and he knew a lot.

Soon we felt as if we had known each other for a long time.

He was two years older. We lived in the same neighborhood so on Saturdays, we would go to the New Market to see animals. New Market was the only place in our city for people selling or trading with their pets. We watched the birds leaping and singing in the birdcages, cats and dogs and rabbits roaming around in the cages, green turtles resting in the mud, and golden fishes swimming happily in the pools. It was more interesting than school or the violin teacher's house.

I wrote to my grandparents every week. I still missed them, but not as much as when I had just left them. They became a sweet memory, a fancy, a dream I had in my mind. I had found a new home, new friends in my hometown. I had melted into the new life.

I played the violin as little as possible. I soon realized why my father urged me to play more than three hours a day, because if I played that long, there was almost no time left for having fun. I certainly refused to do that; I was now eleven years old, and had my own ideas.

3

I became a brave partner in my classmates' eyes after I had beaten Wang Ming. But my closest friend remained Fang-fang, although she didn't agree with what I had done. After I had described the New Market several times to her, she said she would like to go with me someday. "You bet," I said. I was so eager to show her everything that we arranged to go the following Saturday. Liu went with us. I took her to see all my favorite things such as puppies, hamsters, and kittens. On the half way, she stopped in front of a flower shop; there were various kinds of flower in it: roses, chrysanthemums, cannas, and violets.

"Look, how pretty it is," she said. "Do you see the white rose?"

"Yes." There was a white rose standing proudly in a bunch of colors.

"Is it pretty? As white as snow; as proud as a princess."

If I had enough money, I would have bought it for her. She stayed in front of it for a long time.

"It's a good market," she said. "But the Old Market is better."

"You mean the Old better than the New?" Liu asked.

"Yes, it's more interesting."

"Do you know where it is?" I said. "Maybe we can go and look someday."

"I have to ask my Dad. He knows the address."

Her father said he would go with us because it was so big that we would be lost if we didn't know how to go through those narrow alleys. It was really a wonderful place. The first time I saw an alive snake was there. I was quite astonished because it was twisting around the neck of a man. Fang-fang's father told us the man was a snake catcher. The gall of a snake could cure some kinds of disease, and snake soup was very delicious.

There were so many shops and stalls in the Old Market. There were china shops, cloth stores, clothing stores, toyshops, teahouses, and some special stores such as the hairshop, bowls and chopsticks shop, and the walking sticks shop. On the open ground of the Old Market, there was a monkey show. The monkey that could stand up and walk with two feet like a man amused us a lot. After the owner gave the order, it took a bow with hands folded in front, jumped and beat the drum and gong while going around in circles. It teased us into laughing. I couldn't refrain from putting my arm around Fang-fang's waist when we rocked with laughter. But her father looked at me sternly, and I immediately took my hand away.

We walked around and looked at everything. There were too many things to see in one morning. We went to the temple of the town gods, which was located at the end of the Old Market. We looked at the gods that were made of clay but covered with gold paint. They were so tall that I had to raise my head and look up. Some of them were ugly, some of them seemed kind; all were so vivid that they made me change my feeling from dread to comfort. But the most beautiful place in the Old Market was Yu Yuan—the garden which was famous for its exotic flowers and rare trees, the wonderful rockery and exquisite goldfish pool, and the elegant wooden bridges and limpid running water.

After that trip, Fang-fang, Liu and I became so close that we often spent afternoons together. Sometimes we did homework; sometimes we played games; sometimes we went to movies, maybe once a month because we didn't have much money. I loved to play the games. When we met, we never talked about music or played violin. My father couldn't prevent me since he was rarely at home. He was a surgeon who worked in a hospital, and he was very busy. When he came home, he would talk about his patients at our dinner table, telling us how many patients he had received that day and whose disease was serious. I heard this news too often to be interested.

I ate dinner as fast as I could, went right into my room after I finished. I had to stay at home in the evenings. Most of the places in Shanghai were closed after seven o'clock, except for cinemas and theatres. I remembered when I was in Hong Kong, I used to dine with my grandparents at midnight during the weekend. When we left the restaurant, the streets were bustling, everywhere there were cars and people.

Once, I went to Liu's home in the evening. As soon as I entered his room, I found we would have to do everything under his parents' gaze. There were only two rooms for his whole family which included the parents and three kids. Since his two sisters had occupied one room, he had to stay with his parents in the other room. I couldn't enjoy the visit at all and after that, I never went to anybody's home during evenings again.

I was at that time crazy about the stories of Chinese knights, who were adept in the martial arts and given to chivalrous conduct. Wishing to be one of the knights, I waved a stick as an imaginary sword, rode a chair as an imaginary horse when I locked myself in my room. Sometimes, I would ask Liu and Fang-fang to play with me. I preferred to play with them rather than alone, although Liu always vied with me for acting the part of the knight. We used a broom or mop as sword, fighting and shouting while Fang-fang acted the part of a weak girl who was bullied by the evilman. It was a wonderful and exciting game.

One day in June 1966, we didn't play the game when we met. Instead, we went to the New Market because Fang-fang wanted to buy herself a pet. It was a summer day, the sky was blue and the breeze was warm. Fang-fang wore a cotton print skirt and white shirt. The butterfly bow on her hair was white. It set off her black hair and pink cheeks, making her look so lovely.

On the way to the market, we found that Main Street was blocked by crowds.

"What happened?" Fang-fang asked.

"Let me check," I elbowed my way through the crowd. There were some people who had red armbands on their arms tearing down the shop signboards and putting them on fire.

As soon as Fang-fang and Liu squeezed in, a scream startled us. We saw a woman who wearing a light green shirt and black trousers screaming and running towards us. Some guys with scissors in their hands were running after her. She was caught in front of us and surrounded by the people. She was crying and pleading to let her go, but it was no use. Nobody paid any attention to her. The men who were cutting her trousers were busy with their work, and the bystanders watched it with great excitement.

Someone in the crowd said the men objected to the trouser legs. They considered it indecent. It reminded me of the day when I entered the school the first time. I was laughed at because of my shoes. I really couldn't understand why people objected if someone wore a different type of shoes or trousers; but I was too confused to ask questions. We were pushed back and forth by the crowds. Everywhere the things were burning, the smell of the air was awful. There were signboards, clothing and shoes which were taken by force from some of the people. We were so astonished and excited that we absolutely forgot to go to the New Market. When we finally broke free of the crowd we were trembling. Something bad was happening, but we didn't know what it was. Fearfully, we made our way home.

4

Things developed rapidly. The newspaper said that the scenes we saw on the main street were the overture to the Cultural Revolution. The men who had red armbands on their arms were Red Guards and Red Rebels, the vanguard of the Revolution. They were going to clear away the old customs, old moral concepts and old political points of view and build up the new Marxism ideas. All of the old signboards, shoes and clothes had to be burned. My parents threw old stuffs into the fire while I was asleep. In the morning, I noticed that the shoes I brought from Hong Kong were gone. And, the next week, I had to stop playing the violin.

"I can't teach you anymore," my violin teacher told me. "The Red Guards said the private teaching is capitalism. If I still want to teach students, they'll send me to a farm commune." I was old enough to know what he meant. I was taught about socialism and capitalism at school everyday. I knew capitalism was the enemy of socialism and the man who owned his own business or private property was a capitalist.

My teacher sat at his desk. His eyes were dim and his cheeks were gray. He looked very old. "But if I stop teaching, how can I live? My living depends on my teaching. I have to eat, you know."

Only a few days later, the violin became a wonderful toy since it was no use to me. The bow became a sword and the body of the violin became a shield.

One day after school, I was surprised to find the door of my home open. The door was always locked since my parents had to work all day long. I thought maybe our home had been robbed; maybe a thief was turning our things over even now. I rushed into the sitting-room and found my father sitting on the floor. It was a big mess inside. All of our boxes and drawers were opened and all the stuffs were on the floor. Five or six Red Guards were busy searching our house.

"Dad?" I said nervously.

My father raised his head and looked at me. He said nothing but pulled my sleeve; I sat beside him on the floor. I looked at the Red Guards who were turning things over rudely. Some pieces of china were broken, some books were torn. One of them went into my room. I was so angry that I stood up and shouted, "That's my room!"

All of the Red Guards stopped searching and looked at me.

"Your room?" One of them laughed. "We'll certainly search your room!"

"You can't!" I said. "I'm not an enemy of socialism!" The newspaper said clearly that only the house of the enemies of socialism could be searched. My father was a doctor; he belonged to the working class.

"But you're a son of the counterrevolutionary secret agent! You son-of-a-bitch!" one of the Red Guards shouted at me.

I felt ice-cold. A counterrevolutionary secret agent? My father? It was nonsense! I stared at my father, wanting to read the answer on his carefully expressionless face. He looked neither at the Red Guards nor me. I opened my mouth wide, too bewildered to say anything.

I didn't know when they finished searching and left. The door was left open, the house was quiet. My father looked at me and smiled wryly.

"Why?" I said. I had so many questions to ask. I looked at my father, and wondered if he was a counterrevolutionary secret agent.

"Do you believe them?"

I shook my head.

"Right. Now I have to tell you the truth," he said after he closed the door. "Your Mom and I knew it would happen some day. Since your grandparents live in Hong Kong, we have been criticized all the time during last fifteen years. Do you remember when we asked your grandparents to send you home? We were being criticized then for letting our only son live with the capitalists. Your grandparents are considered the enemy of the Revolution because they live in Hong Kong, and your grandpa is a businessman. I'm called a counterrevolutionary secret agent because I've written letters to them. The Red Guards and the Red Rebels think everyone who has a relative in Hong Kong or in foreign countries is a counterrevolutionary secret agent who works for the foreign country against our country. It's not true, you know. You lived with your grandparents for a long time. You know the truth, don't you?"

"Don't be sad, my son. We must look at the future. I believe it'll be corrected sooner or later. Now we have to wait. I'm sorry. It'll be very hard for you from now on."

He was right. I was soon forced to stop writing to my grandparents, and I couldn't receive their letters either. Nobody dared to speak to me in my class; some kids even threw stones, poured water at me. Only Liu and Fang-fang treated me as if nothing happened. After our house had been searched, Fang-fang came to me and said, "I'm sorry, Li Ling. I think something must be wrong."

I really didn't want to cry, but the tears came anyway. It scared her. She put her arms around me and comforted me. I could feel her face near my face and her arms were warm. "Don't be sad. I will be your friend as always."

They still visited me. Liu urged me to play the game and never argued with me again. I knew it was because he tried to make me feel good, but I would rather vie with him for the part of the knight than take it free. During that period, although it was very hard for me, I still thought I was lucky because I had two friends who showed me the true meaning of friendship.

5

Only a few weeks later, classes were suspended in all the school. Teachers were forced to step aside; and students sent back home. Some of them went away to establish revolutionary ties like adults; some took part in the movement and hankered after struggle and criticism. The other stayed at home doing housework, looking after their younger sisters or brothers.

I spent most of my time at home, reading. As soon as the Cultural Revolution began, all the famous western works such as, *War and Peace*, *Sister Carrie*, *Red and Black*, and *David Copperfield* were banned. We were not allowed to read the ancient Chinese novels such as *Travel to the West*, *The Romance of the Three Kingdoms*, and *The Dream of the Red Mansions*, either. The only books we could read were the works of Marx, Lenin and Mao, and the stories about revolutionary wars. But I still could get something I wanted. I borrowed the books from my friends in secret. We covered the books with the red covers and made them look like the works of Marx and Lenin. I read the books with great eagerness when I locked myself in my room, and I gained a lot of knowledge from them.

My father was forced to leave his position after our home was searched. His new job was to sweep the floors in the hospital. The Red Rebels said he had to be reformed through labor. Now he could come home early. My mother and I didn't have to wait for him. He would still talk about his work at the dinner table; however, there was no longer news about patients, but of how many floors he had cleaned that day. He talked about his work jokingly, but I felt sorry when I heard him. My father was a good doctor; he should have been helping patients. He had lost his job only because of the revolutionaries of the new social movement declared him to be a counterrevolutionary.

Liu's father was sent back home since he was a music teacher. Now he could spend a plenty of time with his son. Under his direction, Liu had to practice more than four hours a day. I took pity on him, because he didn't like violin. But he did it obediently. He told me that he didn't want to hurt his father's feelings again when he had lost his job.

We hardly saw each other now, and if we met together, we didn't play games any more. Instead, we shared the news we heard, the scenes we saw, and the articles we read.

One day, I was reading a book at my desk when Fang-fang popped in.

21

"What's the matter?" I asked.

She looked at me and began to sob. Her tears fell like pearls from a broken string.

"Don't cry, Fang-fang," I led her to a chair, and put my arms around her shoulders to make her calm. "Tell me what happened?"

"My Dad is missing. Two days ago, some people came and took him out with them. We haven't seen him since."

"Did he tell you where he would go?"

She shook her head and cried.

"Do you know the men who took your father?"

"I have met one of them before. I think he is my father's colleague. So my Mom and I went to the university yesterday, but they knew nothing."

"Who did you ask?"

"His colleagues."

"I think your father has been locked up by the rebels in secret. In my father's hospital, some of the doctors disappeared. Later, people found that they were locked up. If they really did it, they wouldn't tell anybody. You have to look for him yourself."

"Where do I begin? How can I find him?" She began to cry again.

"Don't cry, Fang-fang; we can think of a way. First, we should call on Liu," I said. "He's full of ideas. Then we'll go to your father's university together. We certainly can find him."

"Are you sure?"

"Yes. We'll do what we can."

We went to Liu's house. His father wasn't home. We discussed the problem in his parents' room while his two sisters were chatting in their room. I always thought that Liu was more smart than I am, although he was just two years older. When he heard the story, he said we had to ask the rebels who were in charge of the university first.

"We certainly can learn something about your father from them," he said. "If he's really locked up, he's somewhere in the university. I can't promise you that we would find him, but we can try."

The main office, which used to be the office of the chair of the department, was occupied by the Red Rebels. They were sitting at the desks, joking and laughing. They had become the leaders of the department because Mao said they were the most important social force. We heard the bad news about Fang-fang's father from them. He was being reformed.

"May I see him?" Fang-fang asked. "I'm his daughter."

"No. Nobody can see him," one of them said coldly.

Fang-fang was going to say something, but she stopped when Liu gave her sleeve a tug. He motioned us to leave.

"It's useless to talk with them," Liu said outside. "They won't let you do anything. We have to find him ourselves."

"How can we find him?"

"First of all, we know he is here," Liu said. "Reform means he is somewhere in the university. Maybe he's locked up, maybe he's forced to do some hard labor. We should look for him everywhere we can."

I agreed with Liu. I believed Fang-fang's father was locked up in the university, because if he was doing some heavy work like my father did, he at least had the rights to go back home every day. I gave Fang-fang my handkerchief for her tears. It would not be good if the Red Guards or Red Rebels saw her crying. We searched along the fences where several small buildings were hidden behind the trees. Some of them were storage sheds, some were machine shops. We looked in them one by one. At last, we arrived at a shed that was well hidden by trees. At first, we thought it might be a warehouse, but we caught sight of a figure disappearing behind the door. We approached carefully, but stopped by a man who was as strong and wild as a bull.

"Get out of here!" he shouted. His eyebrows were thick and heavy over his small, weasel eyes. His pockmarked face looked like a baked sesame round cake.

"We are looking for a boy," Liu said quick-witted. "We saw him running to the house. We are playing hide-and-seek."

"Really?" When he heard this, he became very nervous and gazed around. The pitted face was even uglier than before. At that time, another guard appeared from the door. "Go inside," the Pockmarks said to him. "Pay attention to that old fellow!"

His words reminded me that we had to let Fang-fang's father know we were looking for him in case he was locked inside. I started to shout Fang-fang's name while pretending to find that missing boy.

"Come on, Zhang Fang, I know you're here!"

As soon as I began to shout, Liu and Fang-fang immediately followed. "Get out of here, Zhang fang, it's time for home."

"Don't go near the house!" Pockmarks quickly blocked our way. Everytime he shouted at us, every pockmark on his face grew red.

"We have to find our friend, you know." Fang-fang spoke loudly. At the same moment, we heard a noise inside.

"What do you want, you damned old fellow?"

"I'm not your fellow. I'm Zhang Guang-hua!"

It was Fang-fang's father! We all recognized his voice.

"You bastard! Behave yourself!" The guard shouted inside angrily.

Her father was in that house. Fang-fang was too excited to speak.

"Okay, Zhang Fang, we'll leave. If you still want to hide, go ahead." Liu came to draw Fang-fang and me away. We left quickly.

"That was my father!" Fang-fang said with excitement when we were far from that house. "That's his voice!"

"Yes, I know. But you can't say anything about it," Liu said. "If they know you are his daughter, it won't be good for either of you."

"And Pockmarks will put you in that house too," I said. I hated Pockmarks. We could have entered that house if he weren't there.

We walked home in silence; excited because we had found Fang-fang's father, but sad because we couldn't free him. It was dusk. Liu had to return home to practice the violin. We walked quickly through the paths that wound between the buildings and trees. This was the biggest university in our city. The scenery in the campus was really beautiful, but we weren't interested. Everything was gray and gloomy in the dusk, the trees, the buildings, the mood and the feelings.

6

The big-character posters were everywhere. They blotted out the sky and covered up the earth; the walls of the buildings; the shopwindows; the bodies of cars and the roofs of houses. All of the buses were covered with posters that looked like the moving advertisement billboards. The posters addressed many subjects. Most of them criticized the capitalist-roaders and counter-revolutionaries. Sometimes, when we had time, Liu and I would go outside and look at the big-character posters on the Main Street.

Fang-fang couldn't go with us since her mother was sick. But we would pass by and tell her what we had learned from the posters. Her face became thinner and thinner. Her suffering made me grieve. I didn't know how to make her happy again.

One day, when Liu and I were looking at the posters, we saw a paper stuck on a shopwindow. When we read it, we saw the name of Fang-fang's father. It announced that a public accusation meeting would be held two days later, and the counterrevolutionary Zhang Guang-hua would be sentenced at the meeting. The paper was dated May 17, 1968.

"Do you think it's him?" I looked at Liu nervously.

"Yes," he said at last. "The name is the same, and the university is the same. The paper was stuck here because his house is not far from here. The rebels want all his neighbors to know he is a counterrevolutionary."

At that time, the first thing I could think of was Fang-fang. "We have to keep the secret," I said. "Her mother is sick. They can't bear such a blow any more."

"Yes. We have to. But sooner or later, they'll know the truth, because most of their neighbors will attend this meeting."

It was true, but I hoped that Fang-fang would hear the news as late as possible.

We were so eager to know what had happened to her father that we decided to attend the meeting. When the day came, we entered the meeting-place early and sat in the back. It was as if we were waiting for the court to decide our own future.

The meeting-place was crowded. Suddenly, the lights were turned on and Fang-fang's father was dragged to the stage.

"Down with the counterrevolutionary Zhang Guang-hua!"

"Long live the Cultural Revolution!"

"Long live the dictatorship of the proletariat!"

The Red Rebels, the Red Guards and the audience

immediately shouted the slogans at him. I shivered. The one in charge was Pockmarks.

It was hard to believe that the man standing on the stage was Fang-fang's father. He was wearing cotton-padded clothes although it was late spring now. His face was very pale; his hair had totally turned gray.

As soon as the meeting began, Pockmarks jumped on the stage and criticized Fang-fang's father as someone who attacked the dictatorship of the proletariat by writing books.

"Is it true?" some Red Guards who were standing on the sides of the stage asked.

"No, it is not true," Fang-fang's father said clearly and calmly. "I have not attacked the dictatorship of the proletariat. You can read my books if you do not believe it. In my books, I just wrote the truth . . ." His words were interrupted by curses from the crowd.

"Own up!"

"None of your tricks!"

"Give us a straight answer. What're your crimes?" some Red Guards shouted.

"I refuse to admit to these so-called crimes," Fang-fang's father answered.

As soon as he had said that, Pockmarks, who was standing behind him, hit him on the head and pushed his head down. The ugly face was wild with rage.

"Confess your crimes, traitor!" Pockmarks shouted. I thought I would kill him if I could, but I couldn't. I had to sit quietly as if nothing had happened. I watched as blood dribbled down from the corners of Fang-fang's father's mouth, but his head was still held high. "My words are true. You can read my books. You can't wag your tongues too freely to tell the truth . . ."

I watched the rebels cursing him and striking at him. I watched everything, but I could do nothing. I hated myself. Why wasn't I a real knight, who could save him from beating?

"Down with Zhang Guang-hua!" The rebels shouted. They kept cursing and striking at him. But no matter how hard he was hit, Fang-fang's father refused to admit that he had attacked the dictatorship of the proletariat.

I felt my face getting hot, my hands growing colder and colder. I didn't know when the meeting ended, but followed the crowd going out. My ears were buzzing and my body was trembling. The blood, his proud look, and the angry fists appeared in front of my eyes.

"It's not fair," I said to Liu. "They hit him and poured out a stream of abuse on him, but they didn't let him explain. Why didn't they believe his words? He said they could read his books if they didn't believe him. But they never allowed him to finish nor showed his books to the people."

I had grown suspicious of the Cultural Revolution since my home had been searched. The rebels had no right to search my home just because my grandparents lived in Hong Kong. I had lived with them for eight years, I never heard them saying one word against our country. How could a couple as good as my grandparents be enemies of their country? Fang-fang's father was a famous professor. I saw him working with my own eyes when I did homework at his home. He spent all his leisure time writing textbooks for his students. He never took a day off except when he was sick. A man who worked so hard could not be a bad man. But the reality was that my family and Fang-fang's father were punished, and the rebels such as Pockmarks could do everything they liked.

"I hate Pockmarks, you know. If I have a chance, I'll kill him," I said.

Liu looked at me. "He's just one of them," he said.

I knew. The reason the Cultural Revolution became such a movement was that there were thousands of them.

"They hit him because they couldn't come up with any convincing argument." Liu said.

But why the rebels could ride roughshod over Fang-fang's father, we didn't understand. Why they could do everything they liked while good men had to be punished, we didn't understand. I asked my father when I came back home, and he answered me with one word: "Catastrophe." I thought my father also didn't understand, or if he understood, he didn't want to tell me. But there was something in what he said. It really was a catastrophe for Fang-fang's father, for her family, for my father, for my family, and even for me. I couldn't have fun any more, and I couldn't go to school either. I felt more and more bewildered and confused as I watched the good people being punished and the villains holding away.

That day was the first time we didn't tell Fang-fang what we had seen on the street. When we passed her house, we fled away as if we had done something wrong.

But they soon knew the truth. Her mother's illness got worse, and Fang-fang was shocked and grieved deeply. She loved her father and she couldn't bear for him to be treated like a criminal. She changed so much that I couldn't believe just one year ago she had been a lovely girl who was brimming with vigor.

I was eager to help her, but I was powerless. Nobody could help. Liu and I went to her home less and less because we couldn't stand to see her so sad when we could do so little. But every day I would think of her, and I did my best to find any chance to ease her pain.

7

My father was transferred to another job after he had served as a floor-cleaner for a year and a half, because Mao had called on the rebels to emancipate the people who were involved in trouble due to their relatives. But my father still couldn't return to his original work. He could only be an assistant registration clerk, accepting patients for his former colleagues. He began to talk about the patients again at the dinner table. I was fifteen years old, old enough to know how hard it was for him when he couldn't work as a doctor. I did my best to pay attention to him when he talked.

One evening, he told us about a patient who was suffering a massive gastric hemorrhage.

"He is a professor, a so-called reactionary authority person like me; but fortunately, I have never been accompanied by the Red Rebels. He was sent to our hospital by four rebels. They keep watch on him all the time."

"Is the illness dangerous?" I asked.

"Yes. He has to undergo an operation. He'll be operated on by a young rebel who tries to be a doctor because most of the old fellows like me have been driven away."

"So the operation may be dangerous for him."

"Oh, yes."

"I think his family won't know anything about it," my mother said. She now spent most of her time at home doing housework. Our dinners became sumptuous.

"Definitely not. He was sent to the hospital in a secret way. Nobody knows who he is. I knew his name because I registered for him this morning."

"What is his name?" I asked casually.

"Zhang Guang something, I can't remember."

Zhang Guang . . . I thought, that sounds familiar to me, could it be Fang-fang's father?

"Is he as tall as you, with gray-white hair and a wide forehead?"

"Yes. And very skinny."

"Is his name Zhang Guang-hua?"

"Yes. How could you know?"

"He's Fang-fang's father!" I shouted.

"What?"

"Yes. His name is Zhang Guang-hua, and he is a professor. I told you before that he was criticized and denounced because he had written several books. They said he is a counterrevolutionary."

"Poor man!" My father shook his head.

I was so worried that I couldn't help but think if he died during the operation, what would happen to Fang-fang.

"Can you save his life, Dad?"

"What?"

"Can you save his life? You know, he'll die if he is operated on by a man who really isn't a doctor! Fang-fang's mother has been sick for a long time, and Fang-fang is suffering. They all need him alive. I beg you, Dad, can you operate on him tomorrow?"

My father shook his head slowly. "You know I can't. I'm not a doctor now. I'm forbidden to operate on anyone."

"But you can try, can't you? You can at least ask them to let you do it once. He can't die. You will save him, won't you, Dad?"

"I do want to help him, Li Ling. I want to help every patient if possible. I'm a doctor. I hate to say I can do nothing for the patients. But . . ."

"No but," I interrupted rudely. "You have to save him because you are a doctor. This is your responsibility! You can't try to escape your responsibility!"

"Li Ling! How dare you said that to your father?" My mother said angrily.

My father hung his head. I was sorry for him. But I had to say what I had said. I knew Fang-fang's father would live if my father could operate. At that time, I wasn't old enough to know how hard it would be for my father to do that since he could be labeled a counterrevolutionary again if he wasn't careful.

"Well," he said at last. "I'll try. I'll do my best."

Next day, I waited anxiously at home. The time seemed to pass so slowly that I thought one hour and one year were the same. Finally it was getting dark outside, and I became nervous. I thought I would go crazy if I waited any longer. However, I had to wait. My father didn't appear at his usual time. I was so nervous that I couldn't help looking at the door from time to time. My mother was anxious, too. She had already made dinner—two dishes and one soup—and was waiting for him. The smell of the dishes, the porkmarket lady's bean curd, the pork with vegetable and sanpian soup filled the air of our apartment. These all were my father's favorites. She went to the window and looked outside frequently. I felt really bad. I knew how worried she was. If something happened, she would worry to death. But I couldn't regret, I had to do everything I could to save Fang-fang's father. At long last, my father came. He smiled at me and tapped me on my shoulder.

"Dad?"

"Wait, wait," he put his index finger on his mouth then motioned for my mother, who was so happy when she saw him come back that she hurried to prepare a drink for him in the kitchen, to serve dinner. He smiled at me and his eyes were bright. I felt at ease immediately. I knew everything was done well, although I was still eager to know the details.

He said nothing till we began to have dinner. Since my father was famous for his skills in his hospital, the young rebel who was afraid his operation would fail so that he would lose respect in public, asked him to be his assistant. So my father went into the operating room and performed the surgical operation on Fang-fang's father.

"But he told the public that he was the manager of the operation. When I began to operate, I asked him to give me the blood-vessel forceps once, but he gave me the scalpel!"

"So her father is all right?"

"Yes. Perfectly."

"Can we see him?"

"I don't know. You can try. They certainly will relax their vigilance for several days because he can't move. But you have to be careful. Don't tell anyone that you want to see him. I'll find a patient's name for you to use."

He looked at me with a big smile. I knew he understood what I meant. He knew I would take Fang-fang with me to see her father. I was so grateful that I only said, "Thanks, Dad."

"Hmmmm . . ." my father nodded. He winked at my mother and she smiled too.

8

"Mom, Mom! Dad is in a hospital now." Fang-fang was so excited when she heard the news that she rushed into her mother's bedroom. Through the door, I saw a very big desk set beside a king-size bed. The desk was empty, with only a reading lamp on it. When I did homework with Fang-fang several years ago, the desk was always piled with books and papers. In front of the desk, there was an armchair where Fang-fang's mother sat. Fang-fang threw herself into her mother's arms and cried.

"What did you say, my child? What about your father?"

"He is in a hospital. He was sick, but he's getting better. Li Ling will take me to see him."

"Please let him in."

I entered Fang-fang's mother's room preparing to answer all the questions about her husband. But she asked nothing. She stood up and took me into her arms. Tears ran down from her emaciated face. Her body was shivering. She did her best to stop crying, and exhorted us again and again to be very careful.

The next day we went to the hospital. It was fall. The air was fresh and the sky was a clean blue. A guard stood by the front entrance, but we were allowed to pass because we gave him another patient's name. Behind the entrance, there was a small garden. A cobble road wound from the garden entrance to the ward building. A sign said that the surgical wards were on the second floor. It was so quiet that we could hear our footsteps every time we stepped on the floor. I felt eyes staring at us from everywhere, from the walls, behind the doors, from the ceiling. I held Fang-fang's hand and I didn't know whether her hand or my hand was trembling. At last, we found the room we were looking for.

As soon as we entered the room, we saw a bed covered by a white sheet and a white blanket. Beside the bed, there were two cupboards, a small round table and two chairs. Everything in the room was white including the table and chairs. It seemed so lifeless that I couldn't believe there was someone in it. We moved to the bed slowly and saw him. Two tubes were stuck in his nose, and under the blanket there was another tube connected to a bottle on the floor. The color of his face and the pillow were nearly the same. Fang-fang looked at him anxiously.

"Dad!" She cried out, but covered her mouth with her hand immediately and swallowed her crying.

The head turned on the pillow and the tubes began to

tremble. We held our breath and gazed at him. His eyelids moved. I saw them quivering at first, then opened slowly. They were lifeless eyes and the pupils were dim.

"Dad, Dad," Fang-fang whispered and took her father's hand.

Her father looked at her, but he didn't seem to recognize her.

"It's me, Fang-fang!"

Suddenly, the eyes shone. They became bright. Before I was aware of what was happening, Fang-fang had taken her father's hand and buried her face in it.

"Dad, oh, Dad!"

Her father tried hard to speak, but he couldn't. He noticed me and looked at me. He smiled at me and tried to stretch out his other hand, but I stopped him. We just looked at each other, happy to have found each other.

"Dad, we all miss you. Mom couldn't come because . . ." She stopped. It was really hard for her to tell the truth because she didn't want to hurt her father's feeling. "You know, the hospital just allows two people to visit you at one time, . . ."

A shadow passed over her father's eyes. Tears welled up in Fang-fang's eyes. She knew that her father had known everything. She gave up and cried, "Oh, Dad! Oh, Dad! How can they treat you like this? You aren't a bad man!"

Her father frowned. His eyes were full of tears.

"Fang-fang, don't cry. Please don't." I put my arm around her and tried to make her calm.

"No, no." She threw herself on her father's bed and wiped her father's tears away. "Don't cry, Dad. It's my fault. I love you . . ."

As she spoke, I heard footsteps echo on the floor of the corridor outside. I rushed to draw Fang-fang away and hide her behind me. She was crying. It was easy to imagine what would happen if someone saw her crying.

The door opened. A nurse holding a tray came in. She was about forty years old and dressed totally in white. She was surprised when she saw us. Her black almond-shaped eyes opened widely and the mildness in her eyes disappeared. She closed the door and walked towards us. "How could you enter the room?" she said sternly. "It's not allowed."

She stared at us; and all three of us gazed at her nervously. I didn't know what would happen, but I was prepared to protect Fang-fang. The nurse put the tray on one of the bedside cupboards, and passed by me but asked Fang-fang directly, "Are you his daughter?"

"Yes," Fang-fang whispered.

"Poor girl," she heaved a deep sigh which made me relax a little bit. Then she changed the tone, as if she wouldn't want to express her real feelings in front of us. "You know," she said rigidly. "Your father is a patient. He will be all right as long as he stays here. Don't worry about him. Please go home now and don't come back again. We will take care of him."

Fang-fang looked at her father. His eyes showed that he wanted to say something. He stared at me so eagerly that I couldn't misunderstand his meaning. I looked at him, made sure that he could rest assured. Fang-fang was my beloved girl, and no matter what the situation was, I certainly would do my best to take care of her.

We walked quietly till we were out of the hospital.

"I don't want him to be sick," she said when we left the hospital and grasped my arm. I knew she was scared.

"Don't worry, he'll be saved," I said as surely as if I knew exactly how he would be saved.

She looked at me and nodded. She held my hand so tightly that her body was nestling closely to mine. I could feel her chest heaving. "I know you will save him," she said gratefully.

Yes. I would. I didn't know how, but I still believed that I would.

9

"I have an idea," Liu said when he knew the story. "It's not impossible to get him out of the hospital, but," he stopped for awhile then continued. "You must have someone, maybe a relative who lives far away from our city."

"A relative? My father has two brothers. One lives in Nanjing, the other lives in Hongzhou."

He shook his head. "Is there anyone who lives in the countryside?"

"No."

"Let me think," he said. "I have an aunt who lives in the suburbs of Shanghai; she has a big house. Everytime I visit her, I can get a room for myself. I think she will have an extra room."

"You mean we can send Fang-fang's father to your aunt's house?"

"Yes. The only way we can rescue him is to send him out of the hospital secretly to a place where he can hide. In the city, everywhere you have rebels and neighbors who know each other. If there's a stranger in the house, the informants will tell the Red Guards or Red Rebels. It's much safer in the countryside, specially in the mountain area, where nobody cares who you are and where you come from."

"But how can we get him out of the hospital?" I said. "He is watched every minute."

"Do you know the saying: even the wise are not always free from error? We have to wait for a chance."

It was true. We had to wait. We continued to go to the hospital secretly. Sometimes Liu went with us. He told Fang-fang that his aunt had agreed to let her father live in her house when he could leave the hospital. I wasn't sure if Liu told his aunt the truth. If she knew who Fang-fang's father was, it might be a different story. "Did you tell your father about what we are going to do?"

"I just told him that Fang-fang's father was sick and he needs a place to recuperate; I didn't dare to tell him the truth."

"But he knew Fang-fang's father was locked up. We told him when we found her father in the university."

"Yes, I know. Maybe he already knows the truth. But I think it's better not to tell him." Liu worried about his father would get into trouble if he knew too much. "The rebels don't punish children too harshly," Liu said. "They can't send us to court because we are all under eighteen. They can't lock us up because we are students who belong to school. But they can punish my father."

We all knew what we were going to do was against the new social law of the rebels. We had to take a great risk. Nevertheless, we made the decision to do it, because we all liked Fang-fang's father, and we believed the rebels were doing him an injustice. In secret, we thought it was wonderful to take a risk.

Fang-fang's father was recovering gradually. One day when Fang-fang and I slipped into his room, we found the room empty.

"Where is my Dad?"

"Don't worry, we'll find him."

Just as we left the room, we saw the nurse whom we had met coming towards us. Beside her, there were two other men; one of them was Pockmarks! I felt my body ice-cold, and my heart jumped like deer.

"Where are you going?" The nurse blocked our way and asked. Her eyes were smiling as if there was no one beside her.

"We . . . we are going to . . ." I blushed, and couldn't say anything. I stared at her and started sweating. Pockmarks looked at us suspiciously.

"Sickrooms aren't the playground," the nurse said kindly. "Go to the garden if you want to play." Then she left us and the two men followed her.

"Who are they?" Pockmarks asked.

"The children who are looking after their patient mother," the nurse said.

"Why were they in Zhang's room?"

"Children are mischievous. They can't sit beside a bed for long time, can they?" They disappeared around the corner. As soon as we were left alone, I felt my back wet with sweat. I looked at Fang-fang. She was standing there with a pale face. She was so nervous that she couldn't even move.

"Oh, let's leave here," I said. "We are lucky that Pockmarks didn't recognize us."

"But the nurse knew us; and she lied for us," Fang-fang said.

"Yes. I believe she knows your father is a good man."

"Yeah."

The garden outside was square shaped. There were four thick groves on each side of the garden, one of them was linked with the front entrance. The groves were so thick and dense that they sheltered the whole garden. In the center of the garden, there was a flowerbed with colorful flowers such as Chinese roses and chrysanthemums. Fang-fang's father was sitting in front of the flowers.

"Da . . . ." Fang-fang swallowed the rest of her words as I

pulled her sleeve hard.

We walked towards the opposite end of the flowerbed, then walked around. There were only a few patients sitting between the trees, chatting and laughing softly. After we knew we were safe, we ran to Fang-fang's father immediately.

"Dad, Dad," Fang-fang said. "How are you?"

Her father was so happy when he saw us that he stretched his arms and held Fang-fang to his bosom. Then he gave one hand to me. "How are you?"

"Pretty well," I said. I moved close to him and asked, "Did they just leave you?"

"Yes, they went inside with the nurse."

"Ah. Do they let you out everyday?"

"No. But the nurse said I had to go out like other patients; otherwise, I couldn't recover quickly. I think after several days, I won't be allowed to go out again. They will do their best to forbid me to stay with other patients."

"I see." My mind worked fast. It would be the chance. Whenever they stopped allowing him out, we would lose the chance forever. He could never escape from the sickroom because there was a long corridor and a long staircase. We couldn't have enough time to hide. This would be our only and last chance if we could work it out. I thought with half nervousness and half excitement. "Please do your best to be in the garden tomorrow afternoon," I said.

"Why?"

"We'll tell you tomorrow."

We left him when we saw the two watch-dogs coming from the ward building with the nurse. It was very easy to hide as we walked from the flowerbed to the thicket.

We went to Liu's home directly after we left the hospital. He said he would call his aunt that night and we would leave for the hospital at three o'clock next afternoon—the time to visit patients.

10

That night was the first time I suffered from insomnia. I had thought about more than ten excuses that would get rid of the two guards.

He was sitting on a wheel-chair beside the flowerbed. A breeze stroked his gray-white hair, and the sun brightened his face.

"Dad!" Fang-fang cried. We ran towards him. The distance between us seemed so far away that we ran and ran but couldn't reach him.

"Dad! We are here!" Fang-fang stretched her arms. I felt the wind crying behind me. I ran and ran and ran, as soon as I reached him, it wasn't Fang-fang's father, but Pockmarks!

"Aha, ha . . ." He laughed. "I beat you again!"

"No. You didn't"

"Yes, I did."

"Li Ling," my mother called me. I opened my eyes, felt her hand touch my face. "Breakfast's ready. I'll go shopping now." Outside the sun was shining. My head was so heavy that I couldn't get up as fast as I wanted to. Would we get rid of the guards? If Fang-fang's father wasn't in the garden when we entered the hospital, what could we do?

I went to Liu's house after I finished my breakfast. I told him all the things I worried about.

"Don't worry too much before you leave," Liu said. "The only thing you have to think about is that we *must* win." Although I still worried; I couldn't help it; I knew he was right. We discussed all the possibilities. Because the guards didn't know him, Liu would try by hook or by crook to make them leave Fang-fang's father alone.

"We need to rent a taxi before we go to the hospital," Liu said. "Otherwise, they'll catch us while we are waiting for the taxi."

"Shall we wait for you?" Fang-fang asked.

"I have to see what happens. If I can't get rid of them smoothly, I'll meet you at my aunt's home."

We had never known renting a taxi would be so difficult. Taxi-drivers didn't believe we would need a car. We tried to explain, implore, but nothing happened. At last, Fang-fang told a taxi-driver that her father had to leave the hospital, and she was the only person who could pick him up.

"Where is you mother?" the taxi-driver asked.

"She died a long time ago," she said.

The taxi-driver looked at her, then opened the rear door for us.

It was half past three when we arrived. Liu entered the hospital alone; Fang-fang and I followed. We saw Fang-fang's father sitting in a wheel-chair beside the flowerbed. Two guards were standing behind him; one of them was Pockmarks.

As I watched Liu walk towards them through the thick grove, I remembered the dream I had last night. I remembered what had Pockmarks said to me. I remembered his crazy laughing. My heart beat fiercely. Liu talked for almost ten minutes, then a guard turned and prepared to go. But it was useless if only one left. We saw Liu still talking to them, then they all left together.

We ran to Fang-fang's father as soon as they disappeared into the ward building. We wheeled his chair into the grove quickly. As soon as we reached the grove, we helped him take off his patient's overcoat; Fang-fang pushed the chair away while I walked with him towards the entrance.

The taxi had waited in front of the hospital. We left immediately.

"Where to?" the taxi-driver asked.

"Wang Pu Park," I answered. Near the Wang Pu Park, there were several big hotels; there would be plenty of taxis. We would change taxis there.

"Wang Pu Park?"

"Yes. Our house is just opposite Wang Pu Park," Fang-fang said.

Her father looked at us. I could see he was very nervous. We drove to Wang Pu Park silently.

In front of an apartment building, we let the taxi stop. We paid the driver, then walked towards the building. In the apartment building, nobody would pay attention to strangers. After the taxi drove away, I hurried back to the street and ordered another taxi. It was nearly dusk and people on the street were hurrying home. When we entered the taxi, nobody even noticed us. This time we drove to Liu's aunt's house directly. It was harvest time, and the fields were yellow with rice and wheat.

"So beautiful," Fang-fang's father whispered. "I haven't seen it for a long time." Fang-fang had already told him what we planned to do when I had gone. Now he knew everything.

"When I was a child, I helped my father farming during the summer vacation. I like the fresh air and wide fields in the countryside. Especially in fall, the fields are so beautiful—full of colors, yellow, green, purple and red."

"Purple and red?"

"Eggplants are purple and apples are red."

I was so proud of myself that I felt like a hero. I smiled at Fang-fang, and she smiled back. I hasn't seen her smiling since her father had been locked up.

Not long after the hills appeared in front of us, we arrived at the village where Liu's aunt lived. The taxi stopped.

The village was in a small valley. The green hills were like walls around the village. A narrow, cobbled road was the only contact with the outside. Every house here had a fence and trees. Most of the trees were fruit trees. I saw ripe apples and pears on the trees, a beautiful picture of red and yellow fruit and green leaves. When we passed the houses, dogs tied in front of the doors began barking and jumping. Some people looked at us through the windows, or opened their doors to see what was happening. The villagers were all friendly and kind; they smiled and said hello to us when they saw us. It wasn't like the city where people never said hello to a stranger because they were too confused about who was the enemy to know whether they could even say hello to friends.

It was hard to believe how deeply Fang-fang's father was moved when he met such friendly people. His eyes were wet and his lips trembling. When he said "Hello", the sound was deep and full of feeling.

Near the end of the cobble road, there was a brick house. In front of the house, there were four peach trees, so tall that their shade nearly covered all the frontyard. The door was open. A black dog behind the trees began to bark and a middle-aged woman who wore an apron rushed out and stopped the dog.

"Arhei," she called the black dog. "Come here." The dog ran towards her obediently. She looked at us for awhile then asked, "Are you Prof. Zhang and Li Ling?"

"Yes," I answered. I knew she was Liu's aunt because I had already seen the door number which I had been given by Liu.

"Oh, welcome," she smiled and shook hands with Fang-fang's father and me.

"This is Fang-fang, Prof. Zhang's daughter."

"Fang-fang? What a beautiful name. Where is Jian-guo? Didn't he come with you?"

"Well," I said. "He'll come here soon. He said he had something to do with his friends, so he let us come first."

"When will he come?"

"I don't know."

"All right. Please come in." She led us into the house. The dog named Arhei, seeing we were his owner's guests, wagged his tail and followed us into the house.

The first room we entered was a sitting room, with a wooden floor and wooden furniture. We sat on the wooden chairs around a round wooden table. After we all sat down, Liu's aunt went to the another room and was busy inside. Arhei didn't follow her, but stayed with us. Fang-fang and I played with the dog while Fang-fang's father sat silently. Since he had entered the house, he become quiet. He looked around the room thoughtfully and restlessly.

"Please eat some eggs," Liu's aunt said when she returned into our room with a tray in her hands. She gave us everyone a bowl of sweet eggs, eggs boiled with sweet water. She told us it was a custom to entertain distinguished visitors with sweet eggs.

"Oh, thank you, madam," Fang-fang's father said. It seemed that he knew this custom because he used both hands to receive the bowl and ate the eggs right away. Usually, a guest couldn't eat the food at once when the host served; he had to wait a few minutes to show politeness. But for this custom, the guest had to eat immediately after being served.

After we had finished the sweet eggs, Liu's aunt led us upstairs and showed us the room where Fang-fang's father would live in. "This is the guest room," Liu's aunt said. It was a medium-sized room, about thirty feet long, and sixteen feet wide. It held only a wooden bed, a table, two chairs and a wardrobe. Fang-fang's father walked towards the table.

"Is this suitable for you?" Liu's aunt asked. "My husband said you are an intellectual and would need a table. So I put one of our dinner-tables here. We don't have a desk. I thought having a table would be better than none."

"It's perfect, thank you."

11

Liu showed up about an hour later.

"Where have you been?" his aunt asked.

"One of my friends asked me to help him move," he shrugged his shoulders. "How are you? Where is Hong-hong?"

"She's working with your uncle in the backyard," Liu's aunt said. Hong-hong was her daughter. "What do you want to drink?"

"Hot tea."

"Red or green?"

"Green."

"I'll make it for you." She left us and went into the kitchen.

As soon as she left, Liu told us all the story. "I would never have gotten out of the hospital without the nurse," he said.

When he entered the hospital, he had walked towards the guards and told them that he saw two men who looked like spies in the surgical wards.

"Where are they?" Pockmarks asked.

"I saw them in front of room 205." Room 205 was Fang-fang's father's room. One of the guards became nervous. "Maybe they're looking for Zhang?"

Pockmarks gave him a dirty look, then asked Liu, "Why do you think they are spies?"

"Because they are sneaking around and just don't look like visitors."

Pockmarks thought for a little while then told Liu to go with another guard to the surgical wards.

"No, I won't go," Liu said. He saw Pockmarks' interest was aroused, then added. "I don't want to be killed."

"We had better go together," the other guard said.

Pockmarks looked at Liu, then asked, "Why didn't you tell somebody else but us?"

"Because you have red armbands," Liu said. "I could trust you. And, if they were enemies, you could catch them." So they followed Liu to the ward building at last.

"Why, there's no one here."

"But I saw them," Liu said.

"Maybe they were just looking for a patient."

"Maybe."

They left the surgical wards and found Fang-fang's father was gone. "Where is the old man?"

"Where is he?" They were so mad that they grabbed Liu

very hard.

"Who is the old man? I don't know," Liu said.

"You don't know?" Pockmarks shouted. "You son-of-a-bitch! Are you lying to me? I should have known you before. Do you want to be killed, eh? Then tell me the truth, who let you do it? Who helped you get that old man out of the hospital? Where is he now? Who are you working for? If you don't tell me the truth, I'll send you to the hell."

"I really don't know," Liu said.

"Don't know?" the other guard said. "You said there were two men in front of the room 205. Where are they?"

"I don't know. I really saw them." Pockmarks was so angry that he began to beat Liu. Liu cried as loudly as he could because he wanted to draw other people's attention. People in the garden gathered around them one after another. Some of them asked what had happened and Liu told them the story.

A woman spoke up, "I saw these two men a couple minutes ago. They were visitors of room 207."

"She was a nurse," Liu told us. "After she had supported my story, the guards had to let me go because with so many people there, they couldn't raise hell as they wanted to." He left the hospital, took the bus and came directly to his aunt's house.

"How nice of that nurse," Fang-fang said.

"What does she look like?" I asked.

"She's about forty, and has some freckles on the nose."

"It's her, I believe. I told you about her, do you remember? She helped us a lot."

"Ah!"

We stopped talking when we heard Liu's aunt coming out of the kitchen. Just then, her husband and daughter came in from the backyard with their tools. Liu introduced us to them: Mr. Wang, a good-natured host, Hong-hong, a healthy and pretty girl.

"Today we have to eat earlier," Liu's aunt said when she moved the dishes from kitchen to dining-room. "Because Jian-guo and Li Ling have to catch the last bus at 6:30."

"Me too," Fang-fang said.

"Not you," Liu's aunt said. "You'll stay here with your father."

"Me?"

"Yes. It will be better for Prof. Zhang if you can stay."

"You can help aunt take care of your father," Liu said.

"You two have been hospital several times," he said on the way home, "people certainly know her. We can't let them find any clue. When I asked my aunt if Fang-fang could stay with her father, she said, 'Sure. I've been thinking about that. If she stays here, she can help me doing some housework.' You see, she agreed to take her without any hesitation."

"I guess your aunt knows something."

"Probably. She's smart. I think she knows what's going on."

"What about your uncle?"

"I don't know. He's very quiet. You can't know his thinking from his speaking. But he's an honest man; you can trust him."

Before we went home, we went to Fang-fang's home and told her mother what had happened. Her mother said that two men had already visited her that afternoon. "They said they were Guang-hua's colleagues. I told them Guang-hua was locked up in the university. They said oh, oh, then looked around and asked me where was my daughter. I said she had gone to her friend's home. Then they left. They were rebels. I knew them. One of them was here when Guang-hua was taken out."

"It's good that Fang-fang stayed at my aunt's home," Liu said. "The next time if they ask you, you can say again that she went to her friend's home. I think they'll keep watch on you. But they can do nothing since they have no excuses. Don't worry, everything is all right now. We'll see you soon if we have a chance."

"No, don't visit me, it's dangerous. I'll be all right. I'm so grateful that Guang-hua was able to escape from them. You are my family's benefactors."

"This is something we should do," Liu said. "Fang-fang is our friend. We should do our best to help her and her family."

It was late when we left her home. There was a chill in the air and the wind nipped pretty hard. We buttoned up our collars and walked fast. When we crossed the street, we saw two men rush out of a building and walk behind us.

"We have a tail behind us," Liu said.

"What can we do?" I asked.

"Throw them off," he said.

We sped up, but they walked just as fast. I began to be nervous. My teeth started to chatter. "We can't get rid of them," I said.

"Wait! We have to find an area with lots alleys."

"Let's go to the New Market," I said. In the New Market, we could throw them off easily, because the alleys there were crisscrossed, and the apartment buildings on both sides of the alley were the ideal protective screens.

We sped up until we reached the New Market area. It was not far from our home, and we used to pass it very often. As soon as we arrived at the mouth of three crisscrossed narrow alleys, we started to run. We ran from this alley to another alley, from another alley still to another one. After we had run through five or six alleys, I knew we had escaped from the men.

But we didn't dare to go back home directly. We didn't want to run into them again. We hid in an apartment building and waited; my heart was beating hard while we sat on the stairs.

43

There was a small room beside the elevator which had been the restroom of the lift-operator. Several years ago, whenever I came home, I could see the light of the room which gave me a feeling of safety. But when the Revolution began, all the lift-operators were forced to leave their positions, because the rebels said serving people was capitalism. Now, the small room was empty and the whole building was dark.

"They didn't see our faces," Liu broke the silence at last. "When we get rid of them we will be out of danger."

"We will," I said.

"Are you nervous?"

I nodded. "And you?"

"A little bit."

His hand touched my hand; we held hands tightly.

I felt my body relax and soon I was asleep. When I awakened, dawn was breaking. I shook Liu and woke him up.

"What happened?" He was shocked.

"Nothing," I began to laugh. "I just think we can go home now."

"Oh, I thought that the guys had found us," he stretched himself and stood up.

But I began to worry. "How can I go back home?" I said. "My parents will ask me where I have been."

"You can say you went with me to my aunt's home."

"They won't believe me. If I went with you to your aunt's home, why did I come back at dawn? There's no bus at dawn."

"That's not a problem. We can sleep more," Liu said and sat down again.

"No. We can't sleep here now," I said. "People will leave home for work soon; they will see us."

"We can hide in the restroom." We went into the room and sat down on the floor. The room was empty and full of dust. Liu went to sleep again. I closed my eyes, but I couldn't fall asleep. The smell of the room was awful and the floor was cold.

I didn't know how much time had passed when the bus horns began to sound. I still waited. The people who lived in the building began to go to work. I heard them leaving one after another. Finally, I thought it was time to go home. I woke Liu up and we left the restroom. The building was quiet, nobody even saw us leaving. Outside the sun was shining, we looked at each other and smiled. We were out of danger. We had won the fight at last.

12

Few days later, Liu and I visited Fang-fang and her father. After that, I went alone several times because Liu had to stay home and practice the violin. Fang-fang's father recovered gradually. Half a month later, he could even arrange a walk with us.

"We can climb up the hill today," he said.

"Are you sure?"

"Want a try? I think I can run as fast as you."

"Oh, no!" Fang-fang cried.

"No. I'm just kidding. But I really have recovered. I need to take a walk every day to keep myself healthy."

We climbed up the hills that day. The late autumn's wind was cool and refreshing. The chrysanthemums were coming into bloom along the winding road in the woods. We climbed along the rock steps, enjoyed the birds' singing. The wind made the leaves rustle like mountain bells. We stopped at the top of the hills and looked down on the village. Farmers in straw hats were gathering rice. Hens were busy looking for millet and worms. Ducks and geese were swimming happily in the small river. Only the red placards set up in the middle of the fields showed signs of the Revolution.

"See, the roses!" Fang-fang ran to a grove. There were plenty of Chinese roses in the grove, red, yellow, pink, purple, green and white. The flowers were as big as bowls. People call it the "monthly rose" because every month it would come into bloom. I know Fang-fang like the white rose so I wanted to pluck one for her. But she stopped me and said, "No. Please don't. Dad said flowers are alive and they have feelings."

I looked at her father. He smiled and said. "I told her that story when she was a little girl. I wanted to guide her in taking good care of flowers and trees. But now I really think the flowers are the same as men: some of them are colorful, and some of them are plain. In a business way, a man could be colorful; but in life, I prefer to be plain. I won't bow my neck to influential officials, I won't change myself because of money. If I live, I would live in a plain, but honest way."

"I would too," Fang-fang said.

Her father smiled. "I hope everything will be better soon," he said as he sat down on a round rock. He had changed a lot in the half a month; the sharp and thin chin had become round, the white and gray cheeks rosy, the dull look in his eyes had become bright and nimble.

"I hope so," I said. "My father told me that rebels have stopped research in the hospital now."

"Tell me something, Li Ling," Fang-fang's father said with great interest. "What did they do after I escaped from the hospital? You haven't told me anything yet."

"They interrogated almost everyone in the hospital, especially that nurse. They wanted to know who was the chief plotter. They believed this event might be organized by some kids because they traced down the taxi-driver who took us to the Wang Pu Park, but they couldn't believe that only children could handle it. They thought there was someone pulling string behind the scenes. They wanted to know who he was."

"Did you tell your father the true story?"

"No. I can't."

"You should tell him, he's a wonderful father."

"A very good doctor too," Fang-fang said.

"I know. I will tell him someday."

"Yes, you should. Also, I should say thanks to you. We wouldn't be here without your help."

"Dad, he is so nice to us. When you were locked in the university, he sent us fruit every week, . . ."

"Wait a minute," I said. "What fruit?"

"Yes. Although you never mentioned it, I know it's you. Mom also knew that." Fang-fang looked at me gratefully.

"But I haven't sent any fruit!"

"Really? It's strange. Who would send us fruit except you?"

"Maybe Liu."

Fang-fang shook her head slowly and thoughtfully. "It's really strange," she said. "I thought it's you."

"There are many honest and generous men in the world," her father said. "Since I met with misfortune, many people have helped me. Some of them don't even know me."

We sat on the rocks for half an hour, then went down the hills. Fang-fang wanted to slide down the hillside, so I went with her. We slid down hand in hand and embraced each other when we arrived at the foot of the hill. We laughed and Fang-fang's father laughed with us. He walked towards us and took both of us in his arms.

We walked slowly to Liu's aunt's house. The cool breeze blew gently. The fields on both sides of the road were yellow with rice and green with vegetables. The hills around us were shining with the sun which edged the trees with a golden light. Occasionally, a bird flew in the sky which was so blue that it made the clouds pure white.

Liu's aunt was waiting for us at the dining-room. "Lunch is ready," she said. "Please sit down now and I'll bring the dishes in."

"Where are Mr. Wang and Hong-hong?"

"They are working in the backyard." The backyard was three acres of land that belonged to her family. They grew vegetables on it. During the day, everyone had to work on the public fields, they could only work on their own land during the break or in the evening.

"We'll wait for them. We can eat together," Fang-fang's father said.

"No. They have to spend a long time on the land today," Liu's aunt said. "I don't want your food getting cold."

"What about them? Their lunch will be cold!"

"I'll reheat for them. Now, sit down and eat."

"I can serve the rice," I said. I took four bowls and a ladle from Liu's aunt and served the rice.

"Everytime when I look at them, Prof. Zhang," Liu's aunt said. "I think what a good match they are. I like to see them being together."

"They are only kids . . ."

"So what? In our village, sixteen-year-old kids are betrothed."

"Ah . . ."

As they talked, I was so embarrassed that I couldn't help bowing my head. I stole a glance at Fang-fang, and she was blushing too.

After lunch, Fang-fang helped Liu's aunt clean the bowls and plates. Her father and I went to the backyard. There were many kinds of vegetables growing. Mr. Wang and Hong-hong were watering the vegetables. Arhei was running behind Hong-hong. When he saw us, he wagged his tail and barked happily.

"May I help you?" Fang-fang's father asked.

"No, no," Mr. Wang shook his head as he continued watering. "We can handle it."

I saw that the barrels were empty. I took the barrels and prepared to fetch water for him.

"No, no," Mr. Wang said. He stopped watering. "We'll do it."

Hong-hong grabbed two barrels out of my hands. "It's too heavy for you."

"I can try," I said.

But she took the barrels away from me anyway. She filled them up with water and brought them back to her father using a pole. The pole was on her shoulder, with one barrel on each side. When she passed me again, she asked me, "Want to try?"

"Sure," I said. I thought I could do it if she could. I took the pole from her and tried to carry the barrels. "Oh, my God! It's so heavy!"

She laughed and took the pole back.

"I hardly believe that you, a girl, can carry two barrels of

47

water," I told Hong-hong when she finished working. "It's nothing if you know how to use the pole." "I wish you could teach me some day," I said.

13

"Tell you some news," my father said on our dinner table. "The rebels caught a boy in front of Fang-fang's house today."

"A boy?" I asked. "Who is he?"

"I don't know. I heard the news this morning when I registered two rebels whose hands were hurt. They said the boy bit them when they tried to catch him. He was the boy who had helped Prof. Zhang to escape."

"Are you sure?"

"The one with pockmarks told me that."

"Pockmarks!" I blurted out.

"Yes. He said he saw him several times in the hospital. This time he wanted to deliver some fruit to Zhang's wife."

"Fruit?" I remembered Fang-fang had asked me about fruit. She wanted to know if it was me who sent them fruit every week. "Who is him?" I felt puzzled. "Nobody except us have gone to the hospital," I said. My father knew about me going to the hospital with Fang-fang.

"Who knows, maybe it was a mistake."

"Do you know the boy's name, Dad?"

"No. Wait a minute. Where are you going?"

"To Liu's," I said.

"Be careful! It might be dangerous."

I hurried to Liu's home. He was so surprised when he heard about this fruit-boy story that he asked me twice to repeat it. "Why," he said. "Who is that boy? Fang-fang's friend? We never know that she has such a friend."

"Yeah. And I can't believe there's another person in the world who has been to the hospital besides us."

"That's a lie. Pockmarks said that because he wants people to believe that he has already caught the guy who helped Fang-fang's father to escape. It's his desire to catch someone to mitigate his responsibility."

"But who is that boy? Is he Fang-fang's neighbor?"

"Maybe," Liu said. "Now he's in big trouble; we have to help him."

"I think so. He was hurt. They beat him hard when they caught him."

"Poor guy," Liu sighed. "I guessed that he might be locked in the university right now."

We tried to get some information, so we went to the university the next day. It was winter and the cold wind coming from the interior was so strong that I felt it go through my collar. This time, we couldn't go and search those small houses because we were afraid of running into the guards. We wandered into the school and checked at the posters. We stood beside the students who were looking at the posters too. "Do you believe he is the one who helped Zhang escape?" One of them pointed at the poster and said.

"If I believe a dog can fly."

I gave Liu a nudge. "Shall we ask?"

"Wait," Liu said.

They left one by one when the bells for class rang. At last, only one student remained.

All of a sudden, Liu gave me a nudge. He pointed at the poster and said, "This guy is my neighbor."

"You mean Zhang?"

"Yes. I saw them catching the boy too."

"Really?" the student turned his head and asked Liu with interest.

"Yes."

"Was he sending Zhang's family some fruit when they caught him?"

"Yes."

"I heard Zhang has a daughter who is also missing now; is that true?"

"I don't know. But I don't see her around these days."

"So it was the boy who made two of them escape."

"But I think he is suffering now."

"Sure. He is locked up in the same house where Zhang used to be locked. He is beaten almost every day, because they want to let him confess everything, including where is Zhang now. But so far he has said nothing. I heard that he will be free soon, because there's no evidence saying he is the one who helped Zhang escape from the hospital. None of them in the hospital has ever seen him."

Liu and I went to the university almost every week. Although Liu had to practice the violin, he always could find the time to go with me. One day, when we entered the university, we heard some students discussing loudly in front of the notice column.

"Is that meeting for the boy who helped Zhang to escape."

"Yes."

"Did he confess everything?"

"I don't know. I just can't believe that he could help Zhang."

"Me too."

"So they have to release him at last."

"I think so. Otherwise, the meeting won't be called an education meeting."

"January 20 is tomorrow. Would you go to see him?"

"I think so. I just curious."

We went to the meeting too because we were eager to see that boy. We gazed at the entrance where he would be appeared. As soon as the slogans were shouted, a boy about my age was led from the entrance to the stage. Two Red Guards made him stand at the center of the stage. His face was white and haggard, but the expression in his eyes was unyielding. These eyes were so familiar to me that I started to wonder if he was someone I knew. I knew who he was when I heard his name. Wang Ming. It's him! I certainly wouldn't forget his eyes. They used to look at me with the same expression. I couldn't help but opening my eyes wider and wider. It was impossible I thought, but it was him. It was his eyes, his face. Oh, my Lord! Why was it him? I could remember clearly the day we fought each other in the classroom and I beat him.

14

"What's wrong with you," Liu asked. "What were you thinking about?"

"Do you know who he is?" I said nervously.

"He is the boy named Wang Ming."

"I didn't ask you that. Do you know who he is?"

"Why," Liu laughed at me. "He is the boy who sent fruit to Fang-fang's family."

"I guess you don't know," I said. "Do you remember the guy I beat right after I came back Shanghai from Hong Kong? I told you before that it was the reason why my father made me play the violin."

"Oh, yes."

"It's him. Wang Ming is the boy."

"So," Liu said. "We're lucky. I am just wondering how can we find out his address so we can say thanks to him. Now it will be no problem. You must know his address since he was your classmate."

"Yes. But I prefer that we don't know his address. I was so embarrassed when I found out it was him."

"Tell you the truth, Li Ling," Liu said and smiled. "He hated you because he liked Fang-fang. When you entered your class, you and Fang-fang sat together, and Fang-fang began to get close to you. So he was jealous. He wanted to beat you to make Fang-fang believe that he was better than you. But now I don't think there's any problem if you meet each other again. Fang-fang already has her choice."

"I'm not sure he hated me because of Fang-fang; we were not that close yet."

"Then you were the fool," Liu began to laugh.

I took his word seriously, which made me very upset.

"Don't worry, Li Ling," Liu said. "Now you certainly are Fang-fang's first choice."

"I know that, but I just wonder how can I say thanks to him in the name of her."

"As frankly as possible. I don't think he hates you any more."

We went to Wang Ming's home the day after he was released. It was a small town house located on a narrow lane. The lane was slippery because the road was made of slabstone and there was ice on it. Most of the people who lived in this area were workers. The houses were aged, with dirty gray walls and dark brown doors. We knocked on the door and an old man answered.

"Is Wang Ming at home?"

"You are . . ."

"We are his friends," Liu said.

He opened the door a little bit more and called, "Wang Ming, your friends are here." Inside was very dark.

"Who are they?"

"I don't know." The old man left us at the door.

Wang Ming appeared a couple minutes later. His face was as white as we had seen yesterday, but his eyes were brighter.

"Do you remember me?" I said. We hadn't seen each other since the Revolution started. "I'm Li Ling, and this is my friend, Liu Jian-guo."

"Ah. What do you want?" He asked in an unfriendly voice. He closed the door a little bit as if he was going to shut us out at any minute.

"I want to say thanks to you," I said.

"For what?"

"Because you have been trying to help Fang-fang and her family."

"It's none of your business."

"They feel really sorry for you because you have suffered for them," I did my best to be polite although I was enraged by his rudeness. "They are out of danger now."

"I know that."

"Do you want to see them?"

He looked at my suspiciously. "Do you know who helped them out of danger?" He asked.

"Li Ling and I," Liu said proudly.

Wang Ming turned his eyes to Liu and asked, "How could you help them?"

I told him the whole story and he got so excited. "It sounds like a movie story, isn't? I wish I was one of you." Then he changed his tone and asked me uncertainly, "Do you still hate me?"

"Oh, forget it! I have never hated you before, and I never will."

"But I know you were forced to play violin because of me."

I laughed. "Do you want to see them?"

"You know my answer. Tell me when?"

"What about tomorrow?"

"Great!" He opened the door widely and said, "Why don't we come into my room and talk?" When he opened the door, I saw an old woman who was sitting on a wooden chair inside, sewing. The room was dimly lit. The furniture was simple and old.

"This is my mother," Wang Ming said.

His mother stood up and asked us to come in.

"I'm sorry I can't," Liu said. "It's late. I have to practice violin."

"Oh."

"We can talk tomorrow," I said.

We said goodbye to Wang Ming and his mother and started back home. As soon as we left the narrow lane, Liu asked me, "What do you think about him?"

"I think I start to like him."

The next day we called for him early in the morning, and we took a long-distance bus to Liu's aunt's home.

"What did they do after they had caught you?" Liu asked when we got off the bus.

"Questioned me, beat me. They didn't believe that I only sent some fruit to the family. They said if I told them who was the one behind me and who were the other kids, they would let me go back home immediately."

"Did you see a man whose face is full of pockmarks?"

"Yeah. He is the guy who beat me all the time."

"He's a devil."

"But he can't harm us any more."

"Why?"

"His boss sent him back to the factory because he made the rebels lose face in the public."

"It serves him right," Liu said. "Then why did they release you?"

"They had to. My father went to the university with his fellow workers and asked them why had they locked me up? Because my father is an old worker, because all his companions supported him, because the rebels didn't have any evidence, they had to apologize to my father and release me. So how is Fang-fang and her father?"

"You will find out soon," Liu said.

The village was quiet because all the doors and windows were closed. The winter wheat looked like grass growing on the fields. As soon as we arrived in front of the door, Arhei began to bark. He jumped at Wang Ming and barked loudly. "Arhei!" Fang-fang called him and came out to see what was happening. When she saw us, especially when she saw Wang Ming, she was so surprised that she stopped talking.

"Who's there?" Fang-fang's father appeared at the door.

"Prof. Zhang, this is Wang Ming," Liu said.

"The boy we talked about last time," I added.

"Ah, Wang Ming! Please come in. We so worried when we heard about you. How are you now?"

"Thank you, Wang Ming," Fang-fang said when they shook hands.

"Come on, don't stand at the door. Please come in."

We sat around the table. Wang Ming was so shy that he

hardly opened his mouth. When Mr. Wang and his daughter came back from the fields, he immediately went with them and helped them watering the vegetables. I heard him talking with Hong-hong in the backyard when they worked.

That was really a wonderful day. We worked, talked, ate together, and forgot the old wrongs completely. After lunch, Hong-hong taught us how to use the pole, and Wang Ming learned it faster than me.

"I hate to leave here," Wang Ming said when we left for home at dusk. Through the windows of the bus, we gazed at the hills which rose and fell in the distance. It was dinner time; smoke was curling upward from kitchen chimneys in the village. The sky was gray blue and the fields were wide. Unexpectedly, he turned his eyes to me and said, "You're so lucky, Li Ling."

"Oh, why?"

"If fighting can get what you've already got, I think I will fight with you again."

"Oh. Don't you think that I'm stronger than you now?"

"Ah, not exactly. What do you think, Liu?" He laughed and we all laughed. Then he said to me seriously, "Promise me, Li Ling, you would never forsake her. Would you?"

"I promise," I said.

15

The spring of 1971 was rainy. Almost every other day it rained. The air was full of water, and the ground was wet. At the early spring, I began to go back to school every morning after I had been staying at home for years. Although most of our school time was busy with public-accusation meetings and class struggles, the basic courses such as mathematics and Chinese were given.

At the end of March, I got the first letter from my grandma since the Revolution began. I was so happy that I read the letter several times. My grandma told me that she was going to visit me in the early summer. Early summer in Shanghai was always beautiful and I couldn't wait to see her again.

When April came, the leaders of the university sent Fang-fang's father a mail which said there was a job opening in the University of Anhui Province. If he wanted to get it, he could give them an answer.

"It's weird," Fang-fang's mother said. We went to show him the letter as soon as she got it. "There's not one word of apology. If they made the mistake, they have to apologize. Furthermore, why do you have to leave Shanghai? If they want you to return to your position, they should let you work in your school."

"Yes, I know," Fang-fang's father said. He read the letter again and again. "But I hate to live like this. We can't rely on other people all the time."

He decided to go although all of us urged him to stay. He wrote a letter to the leaders of the university stating that he would accept the position in Anhui, but he would go only when he received the position identification. One week later, he got the identification, so he would leave at the end of April. Fang-fang and her mother would go with him. In my heart, I always had a bad feeling about the whole thing. I just couldn't trust the rebels. I thought it was an evil plan because they wanted to catch him. I told Fang-fang's father about that several times, but he was still determined to go. So I could say no more. Everytime when I saw him busy preparing for the future, I was sad. When the last day came, I had to say goodbye to them whether or not I was willing to. Before I left for home, Fang-fang and I spent hours together at the top of the hills where we had been with her father a half year ago.

It was a rainy day. The rain had just stopped when we arrived at the top of the hills. Everything was so wet that we couldn't sit on the rocks as we were used to. The village below was hazy. The wildflowers spreading on the ground were gaily colored and the drops of rain wet the petals just like dew at dawn.

"Time passed so fast," she said. "I can't believe that I will leave Shanghai tomorrow."

I said nothing.

"What are you thinking about?" She asked but didn't turn her eyes to me. She stared at the village below as if she wanted to see through it.

"I'm thinking about when we can meet again."

"Maybe one year, maybe ten years, maybe never," she said gloomily.

"No! Why?" I caught one of her arms and said. "I will visit you by train when I get enough money. And, we can write to each other while we are separated."

"You will write me letters, won't you?" She looked at me.

"You bet. I'll miss you."

"Me too."

I felt a warm current lashing my body. I held her in my arms and said, "I love you, Fang-fang. I've wanted to tell you for years."

"I love you too." Her head was hiding in my arms when she said that.

I looked for her beautiful mouth, but she didn't raise her head. I hugged her tightly. "When I saw you the first time, I fell in love with you. I didn't know it was love, but I just wanted to see you, wanted to listen to you, wanted to be with you."

"Me too. I didn't tell you earlier because I don't want to get you into trouble. I'm a daughter of a counterrevolutionary; it will ruin your life if you love me."

"I don't care," I said. "We love each other; nothing can separate us. When I was suffering after my home was searched, you went to see me and said you would always be my friend. Now it's my turn to say that."

She looked at me then kissed me on my face. I cupped her face in my hands and kissed her.

It began to rain. The cool drizzle touched our faces softly.

"I'm so grateful that you helped my father out of danger," she said.

"Then what about Wang Ming, are you grateful to him too?"

"Why not. He has suffered for me. Do you know that I thought it would be him when you told me he was caught? I had been wondering who would send us the fruit other than you. When I knew it was a boy, I knew it was him."

"Why? Because you know he loved you?"

She smiled. "But you don't hate him any more, do you?"

"No. We had a talk afterwards. He said I was a lucky man,

and he let me promise never to leave you. I promised him."

"He's a good guy."

"He is. The money he used to buy the fruit for you was his pay for working as a baby-sitter."

"How do you know?"

"I asked him."

She sighed.

"It's good that we have become friends now. Thank God that I beat him once, otherwise I don't know who you would belong to."

We talked about our friends, about the past, the sweet and bitter past. How many things were worth remembering!

"I have to go now," I said when it grew dark. "The last bus is at 6:30."

"Oh, Li Ling, I'll miss you." She began to cry. I felt a lump in my throat, and I embraced her but could say nothing.

The rain continued. My face was wet; I didn't know if it was rain or tears. We stood at the top of the hills and looked at each other. How many words I wanted to say, how many things I wanted to tell her, but I couldn't. Our eyes looked at each other, our arms held each other. It was still raining, and the top of the hill was quiet.

Oh, Fang-fang, how can I leave you! I cried in my heart. Oh, the hateful Cultural Revolution! The hateful rebels.

"Don't forget me, Li Ling," she murmured.

How would I, how could I forget?

"I hope everything will be better soon," I said. "So that you can come back and we can go to the school together."

"I don't know. I can't imagine what will happen if my father gets in trouble again. He will die if they don't let him free this time. He told me that he tried to commit suicide several times when he was locked up. I understand him. How can a man live like a dog? I prefer to die if I can't live like a human being."

"But you can't die! You'll live for me, won't you?"

"Yes." She smiled wryly. "I will."

It grew darker. At last, she held my hand and said, "Let's go. I'll see you off."

We started to leave silently. Suddenly, she stopped and picked up a wild flower on the ground. It was a white, tiny flower. The rain wet its petals and curved its stem.

"I wanted to send you a white rose as a souvenir, but I couldn't. The roses haven't come to bloom yet," she said as she gave the tiny flower to me. "Now I would give it to you although it isn't a rose, and it isn't as beautiful as a rose; but it is white. Do you remember my father's words? The flower is just like a man. I will be a girl as pure as the white flower."

I looked at her when she spoke to me. I worked hard to hold back my tears. I didn't want to cry in front of her. I kissed the flower and told her that I would keep it all my life.

At the bus-stop, she saw me getting on the bus. The rain grew much heavier; she stood outside and saw the bus start. The rain wet her hair and clothes, and the tears wet her face. I saw her grow smaller and smaller, until she disappeared from my sight. The wild flower was still in my hand. It was so tiny that it seemed everything could destroy it.

I couldn't help crying. Outside it was raining.

16

I got a letter from Fang-fang the third day after she had left Shanghai, which said that she and her parents had gotten on a train and would arrive Anhui soon. She mailed the letter on her way to Anhui and she promised me that she would write me again when they settled down. Days passed very slowly; and I had been waiting for her anxiously. One week passed, then two weeks, and I got nothing. I started to worry. I didn't know what had happened to her. I wondered if she wrote me at the wrong address or if the mail had been lost. I would have written her a thousand times only if I knew her address. Finally, I wrote a letter to the University of Anhui Province for information, but there was no answer.

The flower she gave to me was withering. The petals became dry and yellow and the stem turned brown. I put it in between the leaves of a book carefully, so that I could look at it every day when I opened the book. I was sad when I saw it wither; at last, it was as thin as the leaves of my book.

One day, when I back from school, I found a letter on my desk. It was written by my grandma, and she told me she would visit Shanghai next week. This wonderful news made my parents very happy. My mother hadn't seen her since I was ten, and my father hadn't seen her since I was two. They had been counting the dates on the dinner table and discussing all the things they had been preparing for her visiting. But the news couldn't make me happy, although I missed my grandma so much that I would do everything I could to see her. Fang-fang's figure kept appearing in front of my eyes, which quite upset me.

At the end of May, grandma came. We had big dinner the night when she arrived. She was so curious that she wanted to know everything. She asked about the Revolution, about the life we lived, about my parents' work, about my school; and my parents answered her questions one by one. They were so excited that they talked late into night. I listened to them quietly. I just couldn't make myself happy.

My grandma looked at me from time to time when she talked to my parents. When she finally left for the hotel, she asked me to spend a night with her.

It was a big hotel, and room she stayed in was quite nice. There were two beds, a bedside cupboard, and two armchairs. A color T.V. was on a small wardrobe, near a dressing table. On the corner of the room, there was a refrigerator. Grandma opened the refrigerator and got me Coke. It was my favorite drink when I was in Hong Kong.

"Isn't it wonderful?" She said and hugged me.

"Yes," I said. I wondered why I couldn't say anything more than that stupid YES. I wanted to tell her that I missed her, and I wanted to tell her how happy I was now, yet I couldn't. It seemed like a dream to be with my grandma again.

"Tell you a secret," grandma said. She sat beside me and held my hand. "Do you know why I came back here? I want to take you with me back Hong Kong. Your grandpa and I are old now. We need a kid stay with us and help us. It's good for you too since you can go to school in Hong Kong. Do you want to go back, baby?"

I listened quietly. It didn't surprise me. But it was too late. Several years ago, I would have gone with her without any hesitation. How many times I had dreamed that she would come and take me back Hong Kong when I was still a child. But now the dream existed no more. I was used to living here; Shanghai was my home, and I had become a member of the society. Here were my parents, my friends, my teachers, and my dreams. Here I had experienced my happiness, my suffering, my tears and my laughing. I couldn't live without them now. Also, the most important thing was that I hadn't had any news from Fang-fang, and I couldn't leave her alone.

"No, I can't," I finally said.

"Why?"

"I just can't."

She looked at me. "Something must be wrong," she said. "What happened? Can you tell grandma?"

I shook my head, because I wasn't sure if she would understand.

"I know your life was very difficult during the last several years. I read the newspaper every day and I knew everything. If something happened to you, grandma would understand." She looked at me. Her eyes were so kind that I felt I was in Hong Kong again and my grandma was the only person whom I could tell everything. I told her about Fang-fang, told her what had happened and what I worried about. I talked and talked as if I couldn't let myself stop. At last, my grandma stood up and said, "Poor baby, you really have a soft heart. God will bless you." She was a Christian. Whenever she felt helpless, she begged her God to help her.

"Then what can I do, grandma?"

"You should know the idiom," she said. "Good man gets good repayment, bad man gets bad repayment; God repays everybody when the time comes. Fang-fang and her father are all good people, they certainly will get rid of bad fortune when the time comes. Don't worry too much, you'll hear from them sooner or later."

Her words comforted me a lot, although I wondered how long I could wait. We talked for a long time that night. My grandma finally understood why I couldn't go with her, and she said she would wait till I changed my mind. She had never forced me to do anything when I was a child, and she never would.

I fell asleep in the early morning in my grandma's room, and I had a beautiful dream. In the dream, I saw Fang-fang again.

It was a warm day, and the Chinese roses were all in full bloom on the top of the hills. Fang-fang was walking on a narrow path which wound between the roses.

"I'm so happy that I came here again," she said. She smiled at me and I saw two dimples appear on her rosy cheeks. "What about the flower I sent to you when we were separated?"

I took the flower from my book. It was a white rose, and it was in full bloom. The petals were as white as snow, and the stamen was as bright as gold. I gave it to her. She put it on her head.

"I love this place," she said. "Everywhere there is sunshine, and the people are friendly."

I looked at her. The rose was sitting on her head as if she wore a butterfly bow.

"I can't live without sunshine and friends," she said.

The wind was singing. The flowers were swaying in the breeze. She sat on a rock beside flowers.

"Listen," she said. "Do you hear the music?"

I heard the song was singing behind me. It was so familiar to me that I was sure I had heard it somewhere before. I listened to the music. It was coming nearer and nearer.

"Grandma!" I shouted.

I woke up and found my grandma sitting beside my bed, smiling at me. "Did you have a wonderful dream?" She asked.

I nodded.

"Sometimes dreams come true," she said.

I hoped so. I had had a dream and I had seen Fang-fang; she was happy in my dream.

Days passed, then years passed, but I always remembered what my grandma told me. I believed that someday the dream would come true, and I would see Fang-fang again. I kept the tiny flower in my book, and I kept Fang-fang in my heart.

Part Two

A Rose With Thorn

1

I became a grain shop clerk after I had spent three years at middle school. I got no chance to go to the university. Nobody could except those who were accepted by the revolutionary leaders. Liu had been sent to the countryside. I could stay because I was the only child of my parents. During the Cultural Revolution, only one child per family was allowed to be home.

The shop where I worked was near where I lived. It took ten minutes to walk there every day. It was a small, dilapidated, old shop that supplied more than ten thousand people in the area with rice, flour and noodles. Our manager Yan was a short, fat, old man, and the cashier Liang was the only female in the shop—even the cat was a boy.

In Shanghai, people bought fresh noodles and other food when the water was boiling on the stove. So the rice shop had to be opened seven days a week, and none of the clerks could be off on weekends. I took off on Mondays.

From Tuesday to Sunday, I spent more than eight hours a day in the shop, busy with weighing rice and flour in the balance.

One day after I had been working for a month, I got a phone call from the headquarters. A woman who introduced herself as Little Zhao asked me to join a meeting of the Communist Youth League in the evening.

"Who is that Little Zhao?" I asked when I hung up the phone.

"The secretary of CYL," Yan said.

"A woman with a very big mouth," Liang said, who looked at me, making faces behind Yan. "Nobody likes her."

"When I was as young as you, Li Ling," Chen began. He was transferred from somewhere else, and nothing could make him forget that he used to be a man of position. "I used to be a vice-secretary of CYL."

"So what," Liang said. "Now you are a clerk in a teenie-weenie rice shop."

"Oh, come on," Chen seemed to be hurt. He turned to me and explained that he was here because he had responded to the Party's call, supporting commercial departments during the Great Leap Forward times.

"Can't you shut up for a while, the two of you? Customers are coming," Yan said.

Two customers appeared in front of our counter few minutes

65

later; one wanted a pound of fresh noodles, and another wanted fifty pounds of rice.

Chen immediately started to serve the one who needed noodles, so I had to deal with the one who wanted rice.

"What kind of rice do you want?" I asked.

"Long-grained," the customer said.

The counter I was standing by consisted of two containers, one for long-grained nonglutinous rice and the other for round-grained nonglutinous rice. The round-grained rice was a planned supply; every person in a family could buy five to seven pounds a month, according to the season. The long-grained rice was an open supply; but most of people didn't like it, since it was coarser and tougher.

I picked up a big measuring tool and began meting out the rice. The platform scale that sat between rice containers was waist-high. I had to hold my breath to lift the rice on the scale every time I served a customer. I started to lift that heavy stuff, and found it was surprisingly light. Zhang had come silently and helped me to weigh and pour it into the customer's rice bag. Before I could say something, he had already left me for his counting. I realized that I didn't need to say thanks because he had been a henchman of the owner of the rice shop before 1949, and he should do more than others and reform himself by working hard. I glanced over at him working quietly at his table. The abacus sounded rhythmically under his moving fingers.

"Don't you think," Liang yawned behind the cashier's counter, "Li Ling, the routine life of a rice shop is boring?"

"I don't know yet," I said. But it was not the truth. I knew it would be the most boring job I could ever get the day I entered the shop because all I supposed to do was weigh and lift, weigh and lift.

However, I didn't want to complain. I knew I should be satisfied compared with Liu and other friends of mine who were forced to leave their hometown and were struggling in the countryside.

"You will find out sooner or later," Liang smiled. "But then you can do nothing but accept it. It's really a pain when you feel it's so tiresome, but you can't work it out."

I went to the meeting that evening. I was almost numb with cold when I finally entered a big house far away from where I lived. To my big surprise, Little Zhao was a tall, fat, middle-aged woman! Normally, people liked to be called Lao when they entered their forties, because adding Lao before their surname not only meant they were old—Lao means old in Chinese—but also meant they were experienced and respectable. Only young men liked to be called Little.

"Don't be surprised, Li Ling," she laughed loudly. "I'm certainly not young anymore, but I am the head of you kids; and that makes me young forever."

I noticed there were more than twenty young people in the room, sitting around a big table.

"They are all working in the grain shops as you do," Little Zhao said. "I would like to introduce you to all of them tonight."

It was a sociable meeting. I was very excited to meet so many young people my own age. I soon learned that the big house was the headquarters of our company, which had jurisdiction over fifteen rice shops and six sauce and pickle shops. All the young people here were sent to work by the government when they graduated from middle schools, as I had been. Most of them were older than I, having already worked for one or two years.

The guy beside me was a chatter-box who seemed to know everyone in the room. "My name is Ge Qiang. Call me Ge. It's easier to remember," he said. "This is my good friend Liu Fu. I call him Big Liu because he's fat. That guy's nickname is Bamboo Pole; you can see why."

"Who is she?" I asked. A girl who sat in the corner of the room caught my attention as soon as I was introduced to everybody. She had a kind of exotic, unrivaled beauty which made people hard to forget her when they first meet her. She had deep, dark eyes, milk-white skin, pink cheeks and an aquiline nose.

"Her name is Dong Mary. She has been working here almost two years."

"Mary? Sounds so funny. Why does she have an English name?"

"Her father is American. I think he gave her the name."

I looked at her curiously. She sat there as quiet as a marble statue. A beautiful girl, I thought, but certainly not as lovely as Fang-fang.

"She is so quiet," I said.

"Oh, yes. She never talks. She's different."

The meeting ended at nine. Little Zhao told me that the young people's group met every Friday. "See you next Friday, Li Ling," she said.

"See you," I waved back joyfully.

2

The following Monday, I got up at noon. My mother had left a note on my desk asking me to buy some soy sauce and cooking wine so that she could cook dinner as soon as she came back. I had promised Ge on Friday that I would visit him Monday afternoon, so I picked up two empty bottles in the kitchen and left. I hoped I could find a sauce and pickle shop on my way home.

Ge's house wasn't very far, but it was in a different area—an old-fashioned living area where every house had the same style and color.

Before 1949, this area belonged to the middle class and every family had a house of their own. After 1949, more and more working class families moved in, and now it was as crowded as a fish can.

Ge lived with his parents and brother in one room on the first floor that used to be the sitting room for a single family. Because his father was sick at home, I stayed with Ge only half an hour, talking while his father lay in the bed. He was very disappointed when I had to say goodbye to him, because he was very hospitable and loved to talk. But I just couldn't stand to be with a patient in the room and having to disturb him all the time. I excused myself by saying I had to go shopping for my mother.

"Oh, I'll show you where the nearest sauce and pickle shop is," Ge said as I was leaving. "Otherwise, you'll never find it."

The shop was at the end of a small alley. It was very dark, only lit enough to let people see the pile of jars, bottles and pots. The sauce and pickle shops normally sold oil—all kinds of oil; soy sauce—dark or light, as well as hot soy sauce; wines—including cooking wine; cooking paste and pickles. When I entered the store, someone inside asked me if I needed to buy something.

"Dark soy sauce and cooking wine, please."

"How much?"

"One litre per bottle," I answered and put my bottles and some cash on the counter. The price was cheaper if you bring your own container.

She came out of the darkness.

"It's you, Mary!" I was surprised.

She smiled, and took my bottles away from the counter. "What kind of cooking wine do you want?"

"Rice will be fine." I stood in front of the counter; my eyes followed her till she brought my bottles back to me. How inconceivable! She had two dimples too!

"That's your change."

"Oh, thank you." I felt as dumb as a fool.

How could she have the same smile as Fang-fang! I tried to recall the smile Fang-fang used to have so that I could tell the difference, but I couldn't. All I could remember was Mary's exotic smile!

The following days I was suffering. The more I tried to forget, the more I longed for. When Friday came, I felt like I couldn't wait for the meeting to start.

"Hi!" I was so glad when I saw her coming.

She nodded when she passed me by.

I followed her into the house and sat beside her so that I could look at her all the time.

In the meeting, Little Zhao was giving us a speech about how to study Chairman Mao's works while I was looking at Dong Mary. I hoped she would notice what I was doing or only look at me. But she didn't even bother to turn her eyes to me.

"Hi, Li Ling," Ge called me when the meeting was over. "Why did you sit by Dong Mary tonight? Are you falling in love with her?"

"No." I was depressed. "Absolutely not! I sat by her only because her smile reminds me of a very close friend of mine."

"Does she look like your friend?"

"No. Only her smile," I was excited again. "She has the same smile of my friend," I pointed at my cheeks. "With two dimples."

"So what?"

"You don't understand how much it means to me." I told him briefly about Fang-fang, about the relationship between us, and about why we had lost the contact.

"But Li Ling," Ge said after he had heard my story. "I'm sure Dong Mary isn't the same person as Fang-fang."

"I know. But isn't she an attractive girl?"

"I have no idea. Bamboo Pole said she's a bitch."

"Oh, no. Bamboo certainly hates her, I think, for some stupid reasons. I won't accept anyone's prejudice."

He shrugged and argued with me no more.

The next Monday, I got up very early and prepared myself carefully. I took a shower and shaved. I had grown a soft beard since last year. I didn't want to keep it because it made me look even younger.

The shop Mary was working in wasn't very busy. When I got there about ten in the morning, she was sitting behind the counter, daydreaming.

"Hi," I said.

"Hi," she looked up at me but didn't move.

"I . . . I was just passing by," suddenly I shrank. Some guys inside stopped talking. I could feel their curious looks. I worked very hard to keep myself calm. "Ge Qiangs's home is not far from here," I said.

"Is it?" Her voice was cool.

"I'm going to visit him," I kept saying. "We are off today."

"Ah," she said.

"When do you take off?"

"Thursday," she said.

"Can I see you on Thursday?"

"Why?" She looked squarely at me. Her eyes were so dark that I couldn't figure out what was she thinking.

"I need to talk to you," I said. I picked my words very carefully because I was afraid to be refused. "Nothing urgent, but it is very important to me. I hope you will have time . . ."

"If I say no . . ." she narrowed her eyes and looked at me.

"I hope you won't," I started sweating.

"When?" Suddenly she asked.

"Whenever you like," I said.

"Where?"

"You can come to my home, or we can go somewhere else."

"I would like to go to your house," she said.

"Morning?"

She nodded.

Till then, I still couldn't believe it was true. It seemed too easy. Only a few days ago, she hadn't even given me a look when I sat beside her all night.

I flew back like a bird. When I sank into my armchair at home, my brain started to work. How could I get off on Thursday? It's not my day! Liang was off on Thursday, but if she refused to change, what could I do?

"You have to tell me what are you going to do first," Liang said with a cat's smile. "Then I will think about whether I will change my day with you or not."

"I have an appointment," I said.

"Dating a girl?"

"No."

"You can have it," she said and moved close to me. "Only when you tell me who the girl is."

"Oh, come on. I don't know how could I make you believe it's not a date."

"I wish you could," she said. Her eyes narrowed craftily. A cat, I thought, and trying to scratch me. Sometimes I really hated to deal with her. Her voice and ironic smile always made me feel like I had done something wrong. But I hadn't.

"Do you know why I ask you?" She changed her tone, "Because I don't want you to be punished someday."

"Punished? Why?"

She gave me a complacent glance as if she had been sure I would fall into her trap. "Because you're an apprentice. It is a strict rule in our company that none of you apprentices can fall in love."

"Why?" I was now in her trap, I knew that, but I just couldn't help asking that silly question. "I think we are old enough to know what should we do, and what we shouldn't."

"No any reason, only because it is a rule."

I opened my mouth to reply, then shut it again without uttering a word.

"Be careful, Li Ling," she laughed. And the rest of the day, my ears were filled with her derisive laughing.

3

"Mom, I will stay home today," I said when I got up.

"Why didn't you tell me yesterday," my mother said. "I didn't prepare anything for you to eat."

"Oh, don't worry about him," my father said. "He can fix something when he gets hungry."

"I'm not sure if he can cook. Anyway, there's some instant food in the kitchen, if you gets hungry."

"Thanks."

"Please tell me earlier next time."

"Ok. I just forgot last night."

"Have a nice day, my son." My father waved to me when he left.

As soon as they closed the door, I immediately started to clean my room. I made my bed first, then hung my jackets into the closet, and rearranged the books and magazines on my desk. At last, I wiped all the chairs I had in my room, including one armchair and one swivel chair in front of my desk.

When she came, everything was in order.

"What a nice room," she said when she came in. Her voice was like singing.

"Thank you."

"Oh, you have so many books!" she became excited when she found the books on my desk. "*Adventures of Huckleberry Finn*! Oh, I wish I could have it . . ." she spoke to me over her shoulder. Her look was just irresistible.

"You can have it if you like," I said. I would lend her all I had if only she asked.

"Thank you," she sang. "You're so nice."

She wore a bright-colored dustcoat over her cotton-padded jacket. Her hair was done elaborately in two braids. Every time when she smiled, there were two deep dimples shining on her rosy face.

"Why do you stare at me?"

"Ah," I blushed. "I'm just thinking if I have other books you might be interested."

"Do you?" she was excited. "Please show me. I love to read."

"Me too," I said. "I think reading is the only way to color my boring life."

"So do I."

"Is your life boring?"

72

"Oh, yes. I'm always alone. I can't talk to anybody at home except my mother. I have no father, no brothers, no sisters, and no friends because I don't easily get along with other people. I'm a surplus creature in the world."

The sadness in her voice shook me. "No, you're not," I said. "I would love to be your friend if you allow. I'm sure a lot of young people who want to be your friends too."

"Sure. Lots boys want to be my friends. They are attracted by my face, and my body. But none of them pays attention to my soul. Why? Please tell me why? Why don't you think a girl has a soul just like you guys?"

"Oh, please don't misunderstand me," I stammered. "I like your soul as much as I like your face. How can you say you like a girl if you don't like her as a whole?"

She looked at me suspiciously.

"Please believe me."

A faint smile spread over her face. "Let's change the topic," she said. "Tell me why you asked me to come over."

"Nothing important," I said. "I just want to know you and make a friend of you." If I had thought to tell her the truth before she came, I had changed my mind now. I didn't think that she would be happy to hear my story. "Because I could tell that you are a book fiend, too, and we could be good friends."

She was disappointed about what I had said but pleased as well. "I can't believe it," she said. "But thanks anyway if you can lend me some books."

"You see," I showed her my bookshelves. Liu had given me some very good books when he left for countryside. "You can have all of them when you finish *Huckleberry Finn*."

Her eyes shone when she looked at my bookshelves. "Wahoo!" she cried. "*Pride and Prejudice, The Sea Wolf, Madame Bovary*, . . . oh, great!"

"*War and Peace*, that's a wonderful book. I've read it twice."

"Have you? I would like to read them all. Oh, Li Ling, I'm so happy that you invited me here."

"Then show me your appreciation if you're grateful. I'm hungry, and I don't know how to cook."

"Ah," she laughed. "I wondered why you showed me all your treasure."

"Why?"

"Because you're hungry, and you need a cook."

And I laughed too.

She cooked for us, and we had a delicious meal together. She was a good cook, and I loved what she made.

The next day, I went to the shop and asked Liang to exchange our days. I needed to take the day off on Thursday, the same day as Mary did.

"No," she refused me flatly.

"Why?"

"I don't want to be off on Mondays," she said.

"Why?" I knew she was still single, and I didn't think she needed to be off on that particular Thursday as much as I did.

"No reason. I just don't like this idea."

"Can you exchange with me for only one month, please?"

"No."

I was mad. Why was she so stubborn and unreasonable? I had no idea. For a long time, the shop was shrouded in a tense quietness. I knew everyone in the shop looking at us.

"Maybe I can exchange with you," Zhang said, carefully.

"Or maybe you can have my day," Yan said. His was off on Wednesdays. "Thursday and Wednesday are only one day's difference."

"An error the breadth of a single hair can lead a thousand miles astray," she said coldly.

"If I were you, I would exchange my day with him," Chen said. "When I was the vice-secretary of CYL, I often exchanged my days with other people. It's very easy for me to . . ."

"Then you can exchange with him now."

"I will if he wants."

"Be quiet, be quiet! Will you?" Yan always got mad when the two of them started to fight. "Liang, if you can, why don't you just exchange with Li Ling a few times? He asked you so earnestly."

"All right," she said unwillingly at last. "I'll do it because of you, Lao Yan. He can take my day for one month."

The unexpected arrangement didn't make me feel any good because I was so depressed that I couldn't be in the mood to say thanks again.

"Don't take her too seriously," Chen said as we walked home. "She just likes to put us down. There's some history behind it."

"What's the reason."

"Actually, she's a victim of men. She had a boy-friend when she was about twenty. Right before they could be married, the Cultural Revolution started. That guy's family is red, his parents are all workers; but her family was gray, her grandfather was a landlord. So he was faced with two choices: getting married, becoming the target of the Revolution or betraying her and taking part in the Revolution as an activist. You certainly know what did he choose at last. Then she met another man who was her neighbor. Their ages were ten years apart. I believe Liang did refuse him in the beginning, but he had been running after her so long, and finally she gave up and became his lover. Last year, he left her and fell in love with a girl even younger."

"How do you know all this?"

"Little Zhao told me. She knows everything," he said. "When

I was the vice-secretary of CYL, I knew everything too. You know, we all have our family and personal files in their cadres' pockets."

Now I understood why Liang said Little Zhao was a "big mouth". "But they should keep the secret."

"Why? There's no any clause to prevent them from talking. Believe me, Li Ling. In our country, nobody could have any secrets. For example, everyone in our center knows what do your parents do, or where do your grandparent live, maybe as clear as you do. So, just remember my words, Li Ling. No privacy, no secrets. You had better not do anything you wouldn't do in the public; otherwise, you will suffer for it."

4

We went to Long Wind Park, the biggest public park in our city Thursday morning. The sky was blue, and the golden sunshine covered our shoulders, though the breeze nipped at us. The lawns were brown-yellow with dry grass, and the trees were bare. Under the shadow of the sun, the lake was light gray.

We walked shoulder to shoulder, silently. We had been walking around the park since we arrived, neither of us trying to speak. It seemed we were both affected by the quietness of the park. I looked at her sometimes while she kept walking quietly beside me. I wasn't sure if I could talk to her because she seemed to be in an inner world where she would not allow anybody to intrude.

"Would you like to row a boat with me?" I asked her carefully when we passed a small dock.

"Oh, yes," she said.

But it didn't do her any better. She still kept silence while we sat in the wood-boat, rowing in the lake.

"I'm sorry if I'm bothering you," I finally said. "But I should know why do you so upset today. It's not fair if you wrap yourself up with lots thought while we are together. Why can't we share everything, happiness and sadness together? We are friends, aren't we?"

"Yes."

"So can you tell me?"

Her face was pale, "Sorry, Li Ling. I can't."

"Oh, come on."

"I just can't. Please don't push me, Li Ling. Please." She looked at me and her voice was imploring.

"All right. I won't push you. You know, I would do everything I could to help you if only you ask. But you should let me know if you are in trouble. I won't allow anyone to hurt you, do you understand?"

"Yes," she said and smiled at me sadly.

"Now, let me ask you a question. Can you take your days off on Mondays?"

"Why?"

"Thursday is Liang's day and she doesn't want to exchange it with me. So today will be the last time . . ."

"Maybe we can see each other in the evenings."

"Yes, we can. But I just hate to date with you under my parents' gaze."

"Maybe you can come to my home sometimes," she said.

"Are you sure if your parents . . ."

"I have no father," she interrupted me.

"Oh, yes. Ge told me your father is an American, is it true?"

She didn't answer me. Her face looked glum. Suddenly, she put forth her strength to row the boat which made the head of it turn sharply towards my side.

"Sorry," I said and rowed harder to maintain the balance. I was dejected. It wasn't fair that she always wanted to hide something while I talked to her frankly and sincerely.

I rowed the boat with low spirits. I had been waiting so long! I finally gave up to asking her any questions. She could keep her damned secrets! But it certainly hurt me. I didn't think that I would like to stay with her anymore.

The boat was floating on the lake. A slogan pylon stood on the shore of the lake on which Chairman Mao's quotation shone like an incantation: Never Forget The Class Struggle! She didn't look at me, but I could feel she was struggling.

She sighed and stopped rowing.

I turned my eyes to her. She looked at me and said, "I hate to even mention him, you know." Her face mixed with detestation and hatred as she told me the story.

"He was an American officer working for the Kuomintang Government when he met my mother in 1947. He was tall and handsome, and my mother almost immediately fell in love with him after he had danced with her couple times at a party. Soon she left her parents, who drowned themselves into the Wang Pu River when they knew their only daughter lost her virginity and eloped with a foreign army ruffian, moved into his apartment near the river.

"She suffered when she knew her parents had killed themselves because of her in front of her own house. But she sank into the love he brought to her anyway. They lived together almost three years and he never mentioned their marriage. Every time when my mother asked, he always shifted it onto others."

"I guess he was married."

"Yes. But he told my mother he was single."

"How could he keep two families and two women at the same time?"

She was looking at somewhere in front. Her voice was calm and low, as if she was talking about someone else, not her parents.

"His wife was in America. He visited her every Christmas and on vacations. My mother had tried several times to ask him to bring her to America, but he always put her off. My mother loved him so much that she believed every word he had told her. They lived together till 1949, till Shanghai was liberated. After

77

three years together with him, my mother had been used to staying at home so that she had no any idea about what had happened outside. Then one day he told her that he had to leave China for home. It was winter of 1949, and my mother was three months pregnant. She asked immediately about their marriage if he had to leave. She couldn't have a baby without a husband. He promised that he would pick her up and marry her as soon as he settled down in America. My mother believed him again. She was credulous because she firmly believed that he loved her. She was waiting for him while he was flying from Shanghai to Hong Kong, then from Hong Kong to America. When she finally knew what had happened, he had already been gone for a month. You can imagine how difficult it was for her now. No money, no husband, but full in the belly. She started to look for their friends after she spent most of the money he had left for her. It was one of the friends who let her know at last that the one she called fiancé had been married a long time ago and had a wife and three kids in America. She was shocked. She cried but without tears; she wanted to die, yet she couldn't, because she was having her baby. The baby now was her only hope, and she had to live for it. She started to look for a job everywhere in the town. But who would have a pregnant, defiled woman? At the end of her pregnancy, she had to sell her personal ornaments, furniture, and everything she had to get money to support herself. Finally, when I was born, she found a job in a store that kept the two of us from dying of hunger."

Her face was twisted. I was afraid that she would cry, but she didn't. Now I knew why she hated him so much. She never called him her father when she spoke of him.

"But why did your mother still name you Mary? It's certainly a name he gave to you."

"Yes. Before he left, he told my mother, if it was a girl, named it Mary, and if it was a boy, named it John. My mother named me Mary because she thought I was his daughter too. But I know it was because she still loved him."

"After he had forsaken her?"

"Yes. Even today, although she never mentions him any more, I know she still loves him. That's why I hate him so much. He has ruined my mother's whole life; already it's been twenty years, certainly it will be longer, till she dies."

For a long time, none of us could speak. I felt the air was so heavy that I had to cut my breath short.

"Oh, let's row the boat back," she said at last. "I feel so cold here."

"Mary," I didn't look at her. "I'm so sorry."

"It's not your fault," she said calmly. "I should let you know about my family anyway."

"But how could other people in our center know it too? Did

you tell them about your father?"

"No. It's not a secret anymore since the Cultural Revolution started. Neither the Red Guards nor the Red Rebels would let a woman off since her lover was an imperialist, and her daughter was an illegitimate child. After they had searched our house and confiscated our property, they put up a big-character poster on our door on which I was first time to know the truth of my birth," she said bitterly.

"We won't let your mother's tragedy happen again," I said when we left the boat at the dock. "You will be much happier than your mother."

"I'm not sure if I would."

"You will, Mary, trust me."

We stopped in front of a big tree which had a huge trunk and towering branches. My hand was holding her hand, and my heart was full of sympathy. I swore to her that I would do my best to wipe away the shadow of her life.

She didn't say anything. Her eyes looked blank. She seemed to go back her inner world again.

"What are you doing here?" A roar scared me. I turned my head and saw an old picket who wore a red armband standing behind us.

"What's wrong?" I confused.

"Take your hands out of his," he shouted at Mary. "No offense against decency in the public."

She still stood stiffly when the picket left us for his duty. She was deeply hurt, I knew; it was my fault, because I had been so moved that I forgot we were forbidden to show our personal feeling in the public.

We stood face to face, as two pieces of wood. "Oh, Li Ling, why do I always feel so cold?"

"It's winter," my brain was as stiff as my body. "It will be warmer in spring."

She shook her head.

"Please forgive me, Mary."

"It's not your fault," she said.

"But I hope you won't refuse me if I invite you next time," I said.

"No, I won't," she said slowly.

"Really?"

"Yes," she said. "I won't cut my source of books."

"Oh," I started to laugh.

5

We kept in touch afterwards. She was off on Monday now, so we could be together at least once a week.

Since it was the another chance that I could meet her, Friday, had became my favorite day. Every Friday, I went to the meeting early and waited for her to show up. I never sat beside her because she didn't allow me to.

At one Friday night, Little Zhao mobilized all of us to join the Shanghai People's Militia which was a military organization growing in fantastic strength during the Cultural Revolution. "It's the need of the class struggle," Little Zhao said. "We would protect the Central Committee of the Communist Party with our lives and blood if we have to."

"A mobilization order has been issued," Ge said on the quiet. "If something happen, we have to fight with guns."

"Who should we fight with?" Big Liu asked.

"Someone who wants to usurp the supreme Party leadership and the state power."

"Is a someone like Lin Piao?" I asked. Lin Piao used to be the vice Chairman of the Party; his downfall had brought a quake in our country.

"Yes."

"Do we have real guns if we join in the SPM?" Bamboo Pole asked.

"No. We would have guns only in case of emergency."

"How can you know that?" I asked.

"My father is a member of SPM."

"Do you think it's really useful to get the entire nation in arms if it's only someone on the top who tries to usurp the supreme Party leadership?" Big Liu said.

"Who know?"

"I heard that the struggle inside the Central Committee is very sharp and acute," Bamboo Pole said.

"I don't care if the struggle on the top is cruel or bitter, it's not my business," Big Liu said.

"Hush! You will be in trouble if Little Zhao overheard it," Ge said. Little Zhao had been talking impassionedly.

"Why? It's the truth. It won't do us any better or worse if we care."

"But you just can't say it. She's already told you the struggle between the Party is everybody's business."

I saw Little Zhao turn her eyes to us several times, and

every time we shut our mouth up just in time.

She kept speaking, loudly and proudly. But I heard nothing because I had paid all my attention to what my friends talked about and what Mary did. My eyes could never leave her alone as soon as she entered the room. I knew I shouldn't do that, but I just couldn't help.

"Li Ling," Little Zhao said to me when I was going to leave with my friends. "We should have a talk."

"Don't tell her anything about what we've talked." Ge said quietly to me.

I nodded.

"So, what do you think about that?" she asked when only the two of us were left in the room. Her tone was somewhat funny. I could smell the gunpowder in her casualness.

"I think I would like to be a member of SPM," I said.

"I know," she said impatiently. "But what I want to know is what do you think about the relationship between you and Dong Mary?"

I opened my mouth wide but nothing came out. I had never expected that she would ask me about Mary. What did I suppose to say?

"Maybe you would like to avoid my censure; unfortunately, you can't. Because I found it out myself, and it's not just hearsay. So you had better tell me the truth. Have you fallen in love with her?"

"Me? No. We are just friends," I said. I already made up my mind. I wouldn't tell her the truth because I knew Mary and I weren't allowed to fall in love. Not yet; it's the rule.

Little Zhao's face immediately changed. "Only friends? Why didn't you date other girls in our company? Why didn't you go with other girls to the Long Wind Park? Why didn't you row the boat with other girls on the lake? Why didn't you look at other girls during the meeting tonight? Why didn't any other girls visit you but Dong Mary? I think you had better to tell me the truth."

I was standing there as dumb as a wooden chicken while she was speaking like a fighting gun.

"First of all, you should know there's a rule in our company that none of you apprentices can be in love. But if you fall in love with a good girl, I won't say too much because I have been young myself. Now the problem is, you are in love with Dong Mary, who is an illegitimate child of a whore and an imperialist and who will ruin your political life."

"But her mother isn't a whore," I said.

"Who told you that? She did, right? Then how could she explain her mother living with a man and never getting married? Would any good girl except a whore dare to elope with a man in spite of her parents live or death? Li Ling, please to be sober-minded. I am talking to you because I don't want you to be

81

ruined. You are a smart boy and you could have splendid future. Don't you want your future to be ruined because of her? It is your own business if you refuse to come to your senses, but I have to tell you that I'm speaking with you in the name of our organization. So, think it over when you go back home. I know you will be convinced of your mistake."

I could never be convinced, because I just couldn't accept what did she say. However, I knew clearly how important the warning was because she gave it in the name of the organization. Organization in China meant every thing you could imagine. You could fall from the top to the ground because of it; you could attain the highest level in just one step as well. If I refused to listen to her, I knew what would happen to me. I could never go against the organization; nobody could. But I couldn't lose Mary either. I must find a way to satisfy both sides.

"What happened to you, Li Ling?" my mother asked when I entered the sitting room. "Why do you look so upset?"

"Oh, nothing," I said. "I'm just tired."

"Look into the mirror, my son," my father raised his head from newspapers and said. "You certainly have something in your mind."

It's very hard to fool my father. His eyes were just like the scalpel in his hand. They could go through your heart. I sat down beside him on the couch and sighed.

"Tell me what's bothering you?"

"Oh, Dad, I just don't know what to do," I said.

My father was very surprised when he heard the whole story. "I'm glad that you still trust us, although you should have told us earlier. I'm not old-fashioned, and I won't interfere in your private life. But don't you think you are too young to have a girl-friend? When I was eighteen, I was in the college and studied very hard."

"I know. If I have the chance, I would like to go back to school too."

"You will have the chance, if you can strive for it."

"I don't know if I can. Schools are only opened to the kids of workers, peasants, and the Red Rebels."

"It will be changed," my father said. "Believe me, my son, it will be changed. Everything can be changed. You should have known the Great Revolution. Before 1789, nobody in France knew what would happen; when the Revolution rolled up like a mat in 1789, nobody knew it would be ended soon either. A man never can predict anything but he can prepare for the change. You dreamed to be a scientist when you were a boy. Why don't you pick up the old dream and work for it? It will come true if you start to work now."

I was somewhat aroused by the dream of my childhood, and by the prospects my father had described. "What am I supposed to do?"

"Learn something useful, English, maths, physics, even creative writing; whatever you need to learn. It would be good for you whether or not you can enter the school."

My father also wasn't quite sure if I could get the chance to enter university; he acted like he knew something because he wanted to divert my attention from Mary. I thought I finally knew what was his real thinking.

"But what do you think about Mary?" I couldn't help to bring it to light.

"I can't judge her because I haven't seen her. I believe she is a nice girl because I trust your taste. But what can you do if she is a nice girl? Marry her? You can't be married until you're twenty-five. It's the law of our country. Then what else can you do? Do you want to spend seven years in your life to run after a girl?"

Yes, I didn't care if I had to wait seven years in my life.

My father sighed when he saw my expression. "Anyway," he said. "I won't tell you about what you should do or what you shouldn't do. You have to make up your own mind."

6

Liu surprised me when he suddenly appeared in front of me. Under the soft light of the desk lamp, I saw that he had been changed a lot during last three years. Now he was a tall, strong man with brown rough skin, thick chest and wide shoulders.

"Oh, Liu, I wouldn't even recognize you if I met you on the street!"

He shrugged his shoulders and sat down in the armchair beside me. Only when he spoke, I could see the guy I had known for years from the familiar voice. "Ah, you still keep your violin here," he grinned at me. "Do you ever play it?"

"No. I haven't touched it for years."

He shook his head sadly and took the box out of the corner. "I play it almost every day," he said.

"Even in the countryside?"

"Yes." He opened the box and looked at the violin. "What a pity! One string is gone, but it doesn't matter, the bow is still in a good shape." He took the violin out of the box, rosined the bow, toned the strings—all three of them, and started to play. As soon as his fingers touched on the remainders, the room was filled with melodious music, sweet but a little bit melancholic.

I was amazed by his playing. I knew he had kept practicing during the time we were at school, but I still couldn't imagine that he could play so well.

"Wonderful," I shouted when he finished. "What happen? I haven't seen you only three years and you become a specialist! Is that amazing?"

He smiled. "I wouldn't expect that I would be a good player myself."

"Tell me what happened."

He smiled and took the violin again and played it. I stared at him. He had changed so much. He was a stranger now, a stranger who had my friend's voice and smile. The music was curling upward from his hands in my room, deep and sad, driving me into a dreamland with profound mysteries.

"How dexterous your fingers are," I said when it was over. "I can't believe they are yours."

"Maybe you would like to see them clearly," he said, and stretched out his two hands. I was shocked when I looked at them. The wide palms were filled with thick calluses, and the fingers were rough and work-soiled. Oh, Liu! I felt a lump in my throat.

"Now I know," I said to him. "Why you changed so much."

"Do you?" he said casually and went back to his music.

"No, please!" I took the violin off from his hands. "Let it be quiet for a while. You have had enough time to play it in the countryside already, and you don't need to play it all the time when you are here, with me. Please sit down and tell me something about your life." I had already heard a great deal of stories about the urban youth who had settled down in the countryside as Liu had. But the story of my best friend should be more believable.

"What do you want to know?"

"Anything you can tell."

"Nothing interesting at all, you know. We, three of us, live together in a thatched house; work everyday from dawn till dusk, except the rainy days; and go to bed right after supper."

"Why do you go to bed so early?"

"Because we don't have electricity and we don't have enough oil to use our oil lamp."

"What about the local farmers?"

"They are the same. Maybe a little bit better because they live with a family."

"Do you have enough to eat?"

"No. Specially in the early summer, when the new crop is still in the blade while the old is all consumed. We had to gather, strictly to say, to steal some beans in the public field to feed ourselves when we were out of food."

"Poor Liu. You should have told me earlier so that I could save some grain coupons for you."

"That's useless. How much food can you save to support us? We are three, we are hundreds and thousands. Anyhow, the feeling of a belly full of beans is awful. The wind we three break can stink everyone who enters our house away," he laughed as if it was something funny. But I couldn't laugh at all.

"What do you do during the day?"

"Depends on the season. Normally we sow in spring and reap in fall, then help villagers build their houses in winter. They always have some houses to build after fall."

"When do you play your violin, though?"

"Whenever I have time. We three take turns cooking our meals; if it's not my turn, I will have plenty of time to play. And, we don't need to work when it rains. So I can play all day long."

He answered my questions frankly, but I still couldn't be satisfied. I got to know something hiding behind his indifference, "Do you hate the way you are living?"

"What about you? Do you hate yours?" He asked in reply.

"I don't know," I said candidly. "If I could choose, I certainly wouldn't choose my job; but since I couldn't choose, I have to take it without any complaint."

"For me, the answer will be a little bit complex. When I graduated from the middle school three years ago, I was delighted to accept the fortune our government arranged for me. I was, at that time, seventeen, a curious young man full of sap. The outside world seemed to me a changeable kaleidoscope, and I longed to hew out my path in life. I was imbued with ideals and enthusiasm till I arrived the village where I would probably spend the rest of my life. The village made me open my eyes, and showed me a totally different picture from what I had expected and what I had been taught. It is a poor, less developed village where people are living an ancient primitive life. They use oil lamps to light their houses, draw water from river and wells to drink. I was very disappointed when I saw all these; yes, I felt I was cheated, but I wasn't depressed. I childishly believed that our arriving would change them all. I was assigned to live with other two boys who came from different schools in Shanghai. We three started to remake our environment as soon as we had settled down. Only when we went deeply into the society, we found out all we did were wasting our time and energy. The villagers have their own society which resists outsiders. In their eyes, we are domineering urbanites whether or not we have been suffering hunger with them. For us, they are incorrigibly obstinate although they are very kind to us. Gradually, the simple physical labor has lost its freshness. Instead of being curiosity, it becomes a hard burden. Compared with physical pain and the awful living conditions, the boring and tiresome every day routine is more unbearable. We need music, amusement, excitement and adventure; but we can do nothing but work mechanically, from dawn till dusk, then go to bed. You don't know how we felt when we finally understood what was happening. The feeling of being forsaken drove us crazy. I was better than the others because I have my violin, thanks to my father who let me take it. Every time when I frustrated, I turned to it.

"But as you could see, if I hadn't gone to the countryside, if I hadn't struggled and worked at the bottom of society, I would never have fallen in love with my loyal friend, and I would never have found the goal of my life."

I nodded. "So what is your goal?"

"I want to be a violinist, and I want to offer my whole life to music."

"But how can you be a violinist?" A violinist was a professional musician who had to go through a lot of harsh tests.

"I don't know, but I can try. My father said that Nanjing Orchestra would have an opening for an entry-level violinist next month, and I will go and sit for the entrance exams."

"Oh, I wish you a good luck, Liu."

7

Liu left for Nanjing to try his luck right after the Chinese New Year. I waited anxiously for him, hoping he would win. But the result was disappointing. Liu lost, not because of his playing but his parents. A guy whose father was a poor peasant won the violinist position.

"How could you explain it," Liu said resentfully when he came back from Nanjing. "He can only play some of the simplest songs like *Chairman Mao is the Red Sun in Our Heart*, and can't even read a note! But he is the winner, because his father is a peasant, not a teacher, an intellectual, or a capitalist, or anything else! Oh, I really can't believe it!"

In the early summer, I was accepted by the Communist Youth League and the Shanghai People's Militia, became a member of the CYL and a basic member of SPM. The basic member of SPM must be a member of CYL or CCP—Chinese Communist Party, because he should learn shooting and probably would have a gun. Since then, every week I went with Ge, Bamboo Pole, Big Liu and other basic members to the shooting range for target practice.

Mary couldn't be accepted because her background was untrustworthy. I didn't care much about that because I loved her whether or not she was accepted. Now, we never went out for a date because we were afraid of being seen together. We only stayed at home; sometimes she visited me, sometimes I visited her. The more we met, the more we liked to be together. One day, when we were alone, I kissed her.

It was a warm night in July, and the windows of her room were all opened to catch the evening wind. I sat beside her in front of the windows.

"Look, Mary," I said. "Stars are shining. Do you know where Altair is?"

"I don't know, may be there," she pointed at the sky.

"And Vega?"

She shook her head. "Why, Li Ling?"

"In the legend, the Altair is the Cowherd and the Vega is the Girl Weaver. They are lovers, but they can only see each other once a year. Sometimes I can't help thinking that I am Altair and you are Vega."

She looked at me meditatively. "What do you mean? Do you think we should meet more often?"

"What do you think, Mary? I only know I would be fidgety

if I couldn't see you. I love you, Mary. Do you love me?"

"Yes," she answered me shyly. "But I'm just afraid . . ."

"What are you afraid for?"

"My mother always says that a girl may know a man's face but never know his heart. She's afraid that I would duped as she was."

"Nonsense. The time is different, and the men you two met are different. What do you think, Mary? Do you trust me?"

"I don't know. I know you love me, but I'm not sure if you love me as a whole, or only love, as my mother said, a woman's body and a pretty face."

"I told you before that I love you as a whole; I love your pretty face as well as your lovely soul. I love you all. I don't know how can I make you understand that."

"I will know it," she seemed to feel relieved when she heard what I said. "I hope you are the man I expect."

"You will see," I said and I lowered my head to kiss her. It came so naturally that we just held each other and kissed.

"Oh, I love you so much, Li Ling," she murmured.

I didn't answer her but kissed her eyes, cheeks and finally the lovely mouth. It was the first time I kissed her as a lover.

I left for home at midnight, and she saw me off at the door. Her eyes were filled with tenderness and love.

"Bye, my sweetheart." I turned my head back and waved to her. To my surprised, I saw her mother stand behind the window upstairs, looking at us. Her face was darkened by the curtains of the window, but her eyes—I didn't know how could I describe them—shone like a ghost. I should have felt something, but I was too surprised to figure out what it was.

My parents didn't ask me anything the next day; maybe they didn't know how late I came back last night. Almost the whole day, I was immersed in a kind of happiness for no reason at all. I laughed, talked loudly, and made jokes. I knew I was crazy, but I just couldn't help it.

I didn't know how could I pass the rest of the days in that week till the day I could meet her again.

It was Monday evening—we had changed our meeting from morning to evening because summer night was always cooler than daytime.

It was hot. The sun still spread over the ground as if it didn't want to yield to the darkness. The air outside was heavy with humidity, and I sweated all the time on my way. I wore a short sleeved shirt and dark blue pants, the most common style for men in summer during the Revolution. I wished I could wear the shorts.

She was in her mother's room when I arrived, because I was earlier than she expected. My eyes shone when she finally showed up. She wore a beautiful white silken dress, and her eyes were undulated with that charming smile. I had never seen her dressed up like that. "Oh, Mary!" I cried.

She smiled. When I ran to her and kissed her, she just shook off my arms and asked, "Do you like my dress?"

"You bet," I said. "It's beautiful." The dress had a low, lace collar and a wide skirt that set off her soft creamy skin and slender waist perfectly. But as soon as my eyes touched her body, I was shocked. Under the translucent silken dress, her pink nipples were like baby cherries shining with the sun. By the light of the open windows, I could even see the channel of her breasts. I felt a hot current come up from my bottom, and my throat was dry with fire. I tried to calm myself down so that I could take my eyes back, but I couldn't. I was captured.

She turned away from me so that I could see what the dress looked like on her back. When she was turning around, her nipples were dancing on her firm, round breasts like a fire burning my mind. I couldn't think of anything but her. I knew I was acting like a fool, but I just couldn't control myself. She was burning me.

"It used to be my mother's," she said.

"Oh," I could say nothing more than that stupid OH. I looked straight at her. I was tempted, because I had never seen a naked woman before, not even a picture or a photo. The art of nakedness was forbidden in our country even at the time when I was born.

I felt her body touch me, and her breath mixed with mine. I started to tremble; I couldn't bear her touching, I felt I would die if it kept up any longer.

"I wore it today especially for you," her soft voice wafted into my ears and her eyes met with mine. I was very excited when I held her into my arms. "Oh, Mary, I love you!"

She pressed herself closely to me and her body seemed to stick to mine. I held her tightly and felt her stiff nipples erect through my shirt. I just couldn't bear any longer; I had to let myself burn with her. I started to kiss her violently, I couldn't help it. My hands moved involuntarily to her back, unbuttoning her lustily; and my lips touched her fervently on her naked breasts. What a feeling! I cried when I held her breasts with my hands. My penis was up, my bottom was burning. I knew I couldn't wait anymore. She began to moan when I bit her nipples, her body turning round and round in pace with my kissing. Finally I threw her on her bed, pressing upon her.

"Oh, stop!" She cried. She had been trying to get rid of me, but she couldn't. I kissed her impatiently and started to do my business. Now even I couldn't handle it. All I knew was that I wanted her, and I had to have her.

"You bastard!" She screamed and struggled. When I was conscious of the hatred from her voice, my face had already gotten a slap.

"Mary!"

"You bastard! Rogue! Hooligan!" She screamed at me, and tried to cover her naked body with her dress. "Oh, Mom!" She got up and ran to her mother, who unexpectedly appeared at the door.

"Get out of here!" Her mother said to me in her low, enraged voice. Her hands stroked her daughter's hair. "Be quiet, my dear," she said softly. "You will be all right."

"Oh, you are right, Mom, I should have listened to you."

"That's all right, my dear." She seemed to notice right now that I was still there, so she raised her voice and repeated, "Get out! Get out of here, you rogue!"

Mary leaned against the wall, crying while her mother hauled me to the door. I finally gave up struggling. As she slammed the door behind me, her mother screamed, "You will be punished! Believe me!"

"Oh, my God!" I sighed when I was finally on my way home. My ears filled with her crying and her mother's cursing, my body was sweating, my legs were trembling, and my head was hurting.

The past ten minutes were like a nightmare, a horror in which I didn't even dare look back. What had happened? I asked myself. What it was? Suddenly, a thought flashed through my mind. Was that a test? A test the mother and the daughter wanted to determine if the man was a luster or a gentleman short of male hormones? What a preposterous test! It's a trap!

Oh, poor Mary, she was so blinded by her mother who wrapped herself up in the hatred of men. Poor Mary, she didn't even know how to trust a man who loved her with his whole heart. She didn't know that men were not saints; they could never be free from sex. My heart was full of pity when I thought about her. Poor Mary, she was being ruined by her mother, a suffering, hatred-nursing mother, and a father, who could never know the depth of the misery he had brought to his daughter in her life.

I finally calmed down when I went to bed. I thought I was going to help her, because she needed someone to help her get rid of the nightmare.

The next day, I left home in the early morning, and walked directly to Mary's home. There was an avenue right in opposite of her house, green with palms and Chinese parasols. Under the shade of the trees on the sidewalk, a number of old people were having their daily physical training. Some of them doing Taijiquan, a kind of Chinese shadow boxing; some of them performing the sword-dance; and some brandishing a stick. I was waiting there for Mary who should show up around 7:30. Right before the time, she appeared in front of her house.

"Mary! Wait!" I called her name and rushed at her.
She seemed to hear nothing and walking steadily forward.
"Mary, listen to me!" I stopped in front of her.
"Leave me alone," she said, giving me a ferocious stare as well.
"Listen, we should talk that out."
"No. I won't ever talk to you again. Never."
"Mary! You should believe me. I love you."
Without looking back, she left me alone on the street crossing.

I went to work dejectedly. It was the first time I was late, but nobody blamed me. Liang looked at me up and down with her teasing eyes, but didn't say anything. It's good for her to keep her mouth shut; otherwise, I didn't know what would I do to her.

When I had calm down and stood behind the counter, I realized what I planned to do was hopeless. It was impossible for anybody to change Mary's mind, because she had been living with her mother for more than twenty years, and the blind hatred of men had been deeply sown in her mind. But I couldn't give up, I told myself, because I loved her.

When it was dark, I went to her house again. I was still quite shocked when I saw her appear in front of me with burning eyes and stiff face, although I had imagined how she would act when she saw me. She was in great rage. "I don't want to see you anymore, Li Ling! Please leave me alone."

"Mary, let me explain one thing to you; you are prejudiced against me, I believe . . ."

"Prejudiced?" She interrupted me rudely. "Yes, I used to have prejudice, I thought you were a gentleman. But you are not. I have been wrong. Now, I don't have any prejudice against you, and I know you exactly through your own behavior."

"If you mean what I did last night, it's not my fault. It was a trap, the trap your mother uses to buy up your love and happiness."

"Shut up! It's my mother who let me penetrate your disguise."

"You're wrong. She has been corroding your soul by her damned pitiable past; she's ruining you and your life!"

Her color changed when her mother showed up at the door like a ghost from where she had been hiding. I was sure she had been hiding somewhere and heard all we said. "How dare you, Li Ling," she screamed at me. "You will regret what you said today."

"Damn you!" I was really mad. "It's not your daughter's fault or any other men's fault if you have been forsaken by your man. Why do you hate her? She has her right to have her happiness . . ."

"Get out! Now get out of here! I'll never see you again!" She was mad as a beast at bay and pushed me violently out of the door.

The door was slammed in my face, as if at the end of a drama, the curtains fell down. I turned my back to the door and headed for home like a defeated, crestfallen cock.

The following days, I just couldn't brace myself up. When we went to the range for shooting practice two days later, I didn't score any hits.

"What's wrong with you, Li Ling?" Little Zhao was mad at me. She was the company political instructor of SPM in our center. "You should hit the bull's eye as you usually do."

I kept my silence because I had nothing to explain.

"Concentrate your attention in the second turn."

Yet I didn't do it better in the second turn either. I couldn't get interested in it. Anyway, I had hit the fifteen-point ring three times altogether.

Before we left the range for daily work, Little Zhao made a point of giving me a dirty look. She was very mad at me.

"What's wrong?" Ge asked when we were on the way to our shops. "Has she done something to you?"

"Who?"

"Dong Mary."

"Oh, no."

"I can't quite trust her, you know," he said. "I hope she won't trouble you anyway."

"How would she," I said. I didn't want to discuss with him about her right now, although his intentions were good.

When Friday came, I went with a complex feeling to the weekly meeting. I wanted to see her there, although I knew I could never change her mind; but I was afraid to see her, too, because I wasn't sure if she would take my head off in the public.

But she wasn't there. She didn't show up that night. I couldn't help but guess what had happened to her and why she was absent. Her absence bothered me so much that I couldn't have the peace of mind to listen to what Little Zhao was saying. When she stopped me as soon as the meeting was over, I was surprised to see her face was green with anger.

"Sit down, Li Ling," she said. "We need a talk, a serious talk."

I had never seen her so angry before, and I was afraid if it was because of me.

"Did I do something wrong?" I asked carefully.

"You had better ask yourself," she said. "Tell me, why couldn't you concentrate when we were in the shooting range last time?"

"Oh, nothing important. I just didn't feel good that day. I

will be better next time."

"Don't try to fool me, Li Ling. Tell me the truth. What have you done to Dong Mary?"

"I can't understand what did you say," I said. I was confused. It seemed that she knew something; but I just couldn't believe that Mary herself would tell.

"You had better to be honest, Li Ling," she said. "Dong Mary told me that you tried to rape her."

"Me? Rape her?" I jumped from my chair. "What the hell did she say that for? We love each other, and I didn't and never will try to rape her."

"Behave yourself, Li Ling. You are speaking to your supervisor," she said coldly.

I sat down like a deflated rubber ball. Now I had to believe it was Mary who lodged a false accusation against me because of her hatred. I was deeply hurt. She sold me to her mother, only because I loved her. I closed my eyes bitterly and waited for the judgment.

"Then tell me, what did really happen that night?"

I refused to say anything. What could I say? If a girl said that your tried to rape her, that meant you did. Because in our society, virginity of women was cherished so much that none of girls would be willing to frame somebody by casting her virginity aside.

"Don't be so silly, Li Ling," Little Zhao's voice became softer. "You don't need to be made a scapegoat for her."

I opened my eyes and looked at her perplexedly. "What did you mean? Did she tell you I tried to rape her?"

"Yes."

"So what did you mean if I was made a scapegoat for her?"

"It's very simple," she smiled. "I just can't believe what did she tell me. How could I believe a boy, who comes from a stainless family, and who has a clean personal record, would try to rape a girl whose mother was a whore? There must be something more to it than meets the eye."

"So you think maybe she framed me," I said.

"Yes. Did she?"

I was silent. I couldn't deny the fact that she did frame me; but at the same time, I couldn't help but feel sorry for her. Only because she was an illegitimate daughter of a whore—however, Little Zhao believed her mother was a whore, so she had to be always regarded unjustly by other people. What a pity! That's really not fair for her.

"Tell me the truth, Li Ling. If she did frame you, we can settle with her; if you keep silence, that only mean you do admit to her accusation."

"You know that is a false accusation," I said. I certainly didn't want to be incriminated either.

"Then you should tell me the truth. If we don't have any evidence, how can we punish her?"

"But how would you punish her if I tell you the truth?" I asked. I should know what would happen to her before I could make the decision.

"It's certainly a new trend of class struggle in our center; we won't let her off easily."

I was astonished. Class struggle meant that she would be treated like an enemy during the time she was punished in our center. In the Cultural Revolution, it was very easy to imagine what would happen to a person who represented as an enemy: personal attacks, deprivation of political rights and freedom, and endlessly critical denunciation meetings, etc, etc. I could even see her now standing on a stage, being criticized. Oh, no, it would ruin her!

"So?"

"No," I shook my head and said, "I can't tell."

"Think about your future, Li Ling. You will be ruined by your stupid loyalty."

I said nothing.

"All right," she said at last. "It's you who want to be a sacrificial object. You will regret what you decided tonight."

8

Two days later, Yan got a phone call.

"Li Ling," he said when he hung off the phone. "The Party Secretary said you have to go to the headquarters right now." The Party Secretary was the highest leader of our company.

"Why?" Liang asked.

"I don't know. He said Li Ling should join in a political study class for a period of time. He didn't even mention how long it will take." Yan knit his eyebrows when he spoke.

The political study class must be something awful, because all of my colleagues were surprised when they heard the news. Even Zhang who turned his eyes to me from his counting table.

"What happened?" Liang cried.

"Is that something wrong?" Chen asked.

"Who knows," Yan said.

"I really can't understand why they always can find some reasons to set up a political study class. They never care about our basic units. For example, who will work for Li Ling when he leaves for studying?" Liang asked.

"Nobody care these things nowadays," Chen said. "The only thing they are interested in is class struggle. When I was in position ten years ago, we never . . ."

"Oh, cut out your old-sounding talk," Liang interrupted him rudely. "Nobody would regard you as a mute if you would be quite for a while."

But I still didn't have any idea about the political study class. I wondered if it was a class for our young people.

"Shall I leave now?" I asked.

"Yes," Yan said. "By the way, you won't need to come back for help during the lunch time."

We had to take turns to have our lunch every day, and I was afraid they would be short of hands without me. "I can come if you need me," I said.

"No. It's too far away from here to the center. Besides, I'm not quite sure if you can leave for lunch."

What was that political study class? I was puzzled when I headed for the headquarters. What did it mean if I couldn't leave for lunch? Should I stay there all day without a break?

I was led into the Party Secretary's office as soon as I entered the house. It was not the first time I met him but the first time I would talk to him. He was a short man with a very serious-looking face and a frosty manner. He made me as nervous as a little mouse under the stare of a cat.

He was wholly absorbed in talking on the phone, and he did not even look up when I stood waiting in front of him.

"Well," finally he hung up the phone and turned to me. "Now we should solve your problem," he looked up on my face, said. "You certainly know why you are here, and I hope the class will help you clean your mind. During the time you are here, you can't go to work till you can look into your ideological problem deeply."

He talked as if I knew everything, but I didn't.

"Comrade Secretary, can you explain to me why should I . . ."

"Explain? Do you need me to repeat what have you done to a girl? Shame on you!" He tapped on his desk hardly and someone came in.

"Bring him to the class," he said to that guy who was standing behind me. "I hope the class will teach you how to straighten out your mind."

So I turned to that guy. To my big surprise, it was Ge Qiang. He didn't even look at me when he led me out of the office.

We left the Party Secretary silently. Ge walked so fast that I could only follow him. When we climbed up to the corner of the staircase, I heard him muttering, "I knew it would happen someday."

I believed he certainly didn't know what had really happened and I wanted to explain to him. But he had stopped in front of a room on the second floor. "Here we are," he said without looking back.

The door was unlatched. I could see some people sitting around a table, talking. As soon as I showed up at the door, the entire room was suddenly quiet as if everyone inside shut his mouth at the same time. When I sat down and had time to look around, I found out all these people were members of SPM and CYL, including my friends Big Liu, Bamboo Pole, Ge and others.

Little Zhao was there too. She was keeping a straight face when Ge, the member of the branch committee of CYL, was giving the opening remarks. Ge pointed out this was a CYL political study class for the purpose of helping me to deepen my understanding of my thoughts. If I had been confused when I was in the Party Secretary's office, now I knew exactly what was going on. It was what had Little Zhao threatened, something I would regret. I sat there silently. I wasn't nervous as I expected, but I wasn't sure if I could extricate myself from the difficult position either. I knew clearly that I had already become a target of criticism, and they wouldn't let me off easily even if I could get the chance to explain.

"I didn't try to rape her, and I never will," I said after Little Zhao had exposed my so-called crimes in the public.

"Then you should tell us the truth," Ge said. He had been looking at me. I knew he wished that I could clear myself up by telling them the truth.

But I couldn't. The problem now didn't matter how deeply I loved Mary, but couldn't I contradicted myself. I remembered the talk with Little Zhao, and my self-respect wouldn't allow me to change my mind so quickly.

I didn't give Ge an answer. One guy I knew briefly started to rebuke me. He said if I still kept silence, they had to think it was because I committed the offense. Silence was equal to committing; people always said that. His words insulted me, and the feeling of being wronged mixed with pride lashing my heart. I flushed with anger and said, "I told you that I didn't try to rape her, and I never will. If you don't believe me, or if you think I did it, please give me the evidence."

"We don't have any evidence," Big Liu said. "Only two of you know what really happened. Now the problem is, she said you have tried to rape her, and you said you haven't. Who should we believe? If you refuse to tell us the truth, we can only accept what did she tell us."

What he said was reasonable. I should open my mouth, or I had to admit their accusation. At that moment, I realized what a stupid thing I had done! It was I who put myself into such a difficult position in which nobody could help me out but myself.

They criticized me in turn while I sat silently. The formula of criticism was, if I had tried to rape a girl, it's because my bourgeois world outlook hadn't been reformed. It was so ridiculous that even they didn't quite believe what they accused me of. For me, I was quite sure they couldn't do any worse to me because they didn't have any evidence. If they did, the place waiting for me wouldn't be a study class but the jail.

They kept questioning me till lunch time came. I was left alone with a watcher while they all went for lunch. "You can't leave here," Little Zhao said. "We will bring your lunch in."

So I was a prisoner in fact, regardless of whether they had evidence. The watcher was tired of me, so he entertained himself by looking through the windows while I was sitting on my seat.

The interrogation continued after lunch. In face of more and more violent attacks, I gritted my teeth with self-respect and resentment, refused to answer any questions. We confronted each other till evening came, and they had to allow me to leave for home.

My parents must have noticed my exhausted appearance as soon as I came back home. But they didn't question me. We had dinner and my father told us about his patients at the table. When I was ready to go back my room, my mother asked me if I was sick.

"Yes, I don't feel very well," I avoided their anxious looks and said. "I need to be alone for a while."

That night, I couldn't fall in sleep. I looked back bitterly the whole process of my loving affair with Mary which had brought me into such an awful position today. I was so sad when I realized at the end, I still wasn't sure if she really loved me. It was incredible, I knew. But it was true. If she loved me, she wouldn't only trust her mother. If she loved me, she wouldn't frame me. I could never forget the last time we were together, the sexy dressing, the curious acting that was nothing but a trap in which she only wanted to catch me and kill me. I was deeply depressed when I realized this terrible fact. The feeling of disgusting, insulting and injuring had all prevailed over me.

Yet, how could she always act so well? Maybe she could love me if she could get rid of her mother. It was her mother who had killed her real feeling.

They didn't make any progress the second morning either. I didn't want to say anything, and I still refused to answer any questions. When lunch time came, they left me again with Bamboo Pole, the watcher of the day.

As soon as we were alone, Bamboo Pole said frankly to me, "Li Ling, you really shouldn't protect her."

I avoided his eyes because I wasn't sure if I could talk to him when we were watcher and prisoner, not only friends.

"I knew you are wronged because I know her." He left his chair and walked to the door. He closed the door and then turned to me. "I've tried to talk to you when I knew what had happened, and I couldn't get the chance. Believe me, Li Ling, I have been dealing with her for a year and I know exactly what the bitch she is. She's a crazy, out-and-out egoist who can be a vixen if she suspects that you will dupe her."

I knew he was right. But I still had pity on her, and that it was her mother who had poisoned her mind. "Do you ever read Dickens' *Great Expectations*?" I asked him. "I think her mother is the arch-criminal."

He shook his head. "I haven't read the book. Let's come to the subject again. I don't know what did really happen between two of you, but I trust you. You shouldn't ruin yourself by being partial to her. You should clear yourself."

"I know. I have to; otherwise, you'll think I'm a rapist."

"No. I won't. I know you, and I believe you are innocent. But most of people here don't. They don't know you, and they can't trust you if you don't show them the truth."

So I finally told them the truth and was allowed to return to the shop two days later.

9

The shop didn't change any but I was changed. First of all, I wasn't a stainless young man anymore. In the company, I could hear the gossip everywhere that I had intended to rape a girl who wanted to refuse my advances; and I had been in the political study class and been criticized. Although I was cleared of the rape charge, I still had a bad record in people's mind. It was always the same if someone did something, or tried to do something, or didn't do anything but mistakenly believed he did something for any reasons. Sometimes when I met some silly girls in our company, they fled as if they had seen a ghost or a dangerous criminal who would rape them on the street.

I suffered; but I didn't feel worse when I got a phone call from Little Zhao the second day I was back. She informed me that I wouldn't need to go shooting anymore, because I had been expelled from the SPM. She didn't give me any reason, but I knew. It was the result of the political study meeting, and a part of her threat.

I became very reticent. I never talked, but worked from morning till evening. My colleagues didn't treat me bad—Zhang even helped me more than ever because he thought I was his company now, but I just didn't feel like I could talk to them. It kept on like this till one day Chen couldn't bear his burning curiosity anymore.

"Someone asked me about you yesterday," he said when we stood together behind the counter in the early afternoon. The shop was quiet. Yan had left for bank and Zhang was off that day. "Almost every day I'm asked."

"Then you should be tired of asking people yourself," Liang said.

"Oh, yes. But I think I should know something because I have been working with him."

"If I were you, I wouldn't ask," she said.

"Would you? I just can't control myself. I want to know the truth because I can't believe what did people told me."

I could feel two of them looking at me and waiting for my answer. If I were they, I would be the same. Why they couldn't know what had happened to their colleague? They had been working with him all the time, and treated him like a brother. I knew I should let them know something, or at least let them know what was my attitude to that all-mixed-up tale. So I did.

"She should be punished," Liang's reaction was very

99

extreme. "If there's any justice in the world."

"I understand you, Li Ling," Chen said. "You are a man."

But most of people in our company didn't think I was a man. They avoided me as if I were a villain. When Friday came, I had a hard time deciding whether to go to the weekly meeting. I could imagine what it would be if I went there: eyes of spite, whispers among the people, and curious stares from everywhere. But, if I refused to go, it would be even worse. It would be the best reason to make them believe I was guilty. Otherwise, why should I be afraid to go?

I was there a little bit early so that I could take a seat in a corner. I didn't want to be too noticeable. People came in twos and threes; they seemed to notice I was there immediately and bypassed me carefully. I saw Ge coming, he hesitated for a while, then sat far away from me in the crowd. So did Bamboo Pole. When Big Liu came, I simply lowered my head and shut my eyes. Soon the corner I was sitting became the most conspicuous place because only me who was there. I felt like I was sitting on a bed of nails and tenterhooks and everyone in the room was looking at me.

I didn't know how it ended when I was left alone in the room. I was numb with dejection and walked slowly to my home. The sky was dark and the streetlights were dim. I was all alone and my heart was bleeding. Oh, why? Why had they done me so unjustly? I didn't do anything shameful, anything scandalous!

"Li Ling!" Someone called me.

On the corner of the street, there were some people waving at me, one of them was walking towards me. It's Ge. "I'm sorry," he said when he stopped in front of me. "What a shame that we couldn't speak to you in public." He was very disturbed, and he didn't lift his eyes when he spoke to me. "I'm awfully sorry."

"We are still your friends, Li Ling," Bamboo Pole said. "Believe me."

"I know," I said. I felt a lump in my throat. I wouldn't blame them because I knew what they did tonight was against their will. They were forced to show that they didn't implicate in my scandal. I understood them. But I just couldn't accept the fact that I was a culprit now.

"Don't be so disheartened, Li Ling. The rumor will die away somedays. It only needs time," Big Liu said.

"You can stay at home," Ge said. "Till people forget what they heard and find out you were framed."

After I had been insulted like that? No way! "I certainly won't go the meeting anymore after tonight," I said.

"We must let Dong Mary pay the price," Bamboo Pole said. He now hated her more than ever.

"We won't let her off, believe me," Ge said.

They all hated her; now even myself. She had gone too far! Not long after I had been expelled from SPM, I got a disciplinary action within the CYL although I could keep my membership, at least. As a member of the branch committee of CYL, Ge had persuaded Little Zhao and the Party Secretary to withdraw a proposal of expelling me from membership.

Blows came upon to me one after another; I knew clearly now that I had to suffer so long as I stayed in the company. But how could I change my job? In China, nothing was more difficult than changing a job. Nobody in the company, except a few who transferred because of cadre's will, could ever change his job. People had to work from the day they entered till the day they retired. No change, no transfer. Once you had a job, whatever it was, whether or not you liked it, you had to keep it till you were old.

At that time, I got a letter from Liu. He was still full of ideals, dreaming of being a violinist. He said he would go to Peking next month because a conservatory of music there would give an entrance exam to the public. Now his goal was to be a student at the conservatory. I was excited when I finished reading. Was it the best way for me too, to be a student?

The University was opened wider than before. Some of the other kids, the children of teachers, doctors, or whatever could be accepted. But the number was limited. If 90% of the freshmen were the kids of workers and peasants, only 10% of the freshmen could be someone like me. Of course, it would be much harder for me if I wanted to enter the university. But it was the only chance if I wanted to change my life.

My parents became my best allies when I told them what I was going to do. My father picked up the textbooks for me and taught me himself.

All my friends stood by me when they knew my plan. Ge, Bamboo Pole and Big Liu did their best to find me the books I needed in the used-book stores, at the house of their friends, or in the stalls of the market, because there's no more useful textbooks in the reformed bookstores. They visited me, letting me know what was happening in our company. As time passed, we became closer and closer. That was an unexpected result of my tragedy and it comforted me a lot.

Liu lost again in Peking, but he didn't lose his faith in his goal. He said he would arrange a competition between us and see who would be the first to achieve his goal. Now I felt like a horse, kept running on my way at full speed.

He made his first step sooner than I did. The county where he lived had a music band, and he was elected by a county cadre as a member. A country music band could only play some simple songs for entertaining the farmers, but Liu still felt like a king, because he finally became a violinist, no matter what it really was.

He was back in Shanghai once after he had gotten the order for his transfer. We didn't talk much, though, because I was very busy. I had been preparing for the entrance exam.

When the day came, I went to the university full of self-confidence. I was sure I would get good points in any case because I had prepared more than I needed to.

I got one of the highest scores that year in our city. My parents were so glad that they told me from now on I could set my mind at rest and wait. At their time, good points meant the admission of a good school.

But how could I set my mind at rest? Waiting was sometimes a kind of suffering, especially when I finally had some hope for the future. From the day I knew my scores till the day I knew the result, I was as restless as an ant on a hot pan.

We, my parents and I, as well as my friends, were all shocked when we finally knew the result: I was refused. The reason for refusing me was very simple. I had bourgeois ideas—the most terrible charge at that time.

"We've done our best," the man in the admission office told me. "Because of your scores, we did want to accept you as a freshman. I've called your company several times, but your company refused to sign the permission. At last, they put their reasons before us, and we had to give up."

"What is the reason?"

His eyes looked at me curiously. "They said you had bourgeois ideas, and you had tried to rape a girl once in your company."

"No!" I cried. "It's not true!"

"But what could we do? They even showed us the records of the political study class."

So, I failed. More than that, I finally knew, after working so hard for half a year, that all my wishes were fruitless, like drawing water with a bamboo basket—all in vain.

I couldn't remember how was I able to walk back after I had realized my fatal failure. I could only remember that I had lain on my bed for several days afterwards. My parents didn't disturb me when I was hiding in my room, trying to recover. Only when I got up from the bed couple days later, they asked me if I still wanted to learn something.

What could I do if I didn't spend some time on books? I had no choice.

My failure, like a black cloud, weighed down my heart and spirit. It wasn't because I was too weak to suffer another setback, but because I was too clear-headed to ignore the truth: I could never change my fate unless something happened. I was defeated by an organization which could control everybody's fortune and life. I could never break away from it no matter how hard I struggled.

I fell to the books again although I had lost my goal. As the days passed, study became something that I did automatically every day. Only when my friends came to visit me, would I put down my book for a while and talk to them.

"She's transferred to another company, you know." One day, Ge told me.

"Who?"

"Dong Mary," Bamboo Pole said. "She's gone."

"She can't stay here anymore," Ge said with pleasure. "Now everyone knows she has seduced you and she is a bitch. She's lost her face in the public."

They reminded me of the story Liang had told me one day when I was at the shop. She said she had met Mary on the street, and Mary had run away from her as a frightened stray cur.

"What have you done to her?" I asked.

"I just asked her what had she done to you," Liang told me. "She got surprised and asked me who I was and who was I talking about."

"What did you say?"

"I said I was the one who knew the truth. I knew that she's scurrilously hurt a man who loved her. I said there would be a judgment on her for her shameless behavior; and she could never escape from punishment."

"You shouldn't do that," I said.

"But I want to make a reprisal for you," she said. "I've been hurt by my lover twice, and I know what you felt about her."

"Where did she transfer?"

"Somewhere in the suburbs. Now she has to take three buses every day to go to work," Ge said.

"Poor Mary."

"Why? She's hurt you so hard! She is the one who's ruined your whole life!"

What could I say? I was ruined. But it wouldn't be any better for me if she was punished. The two of us were only moths in our society; no matter how hard we worked, we could never handle our own lives.

10

At the beginning of 1976, the death of Primier Zhou brought an unexpected violent storm to the whole country, stirring up the stagnant pool with an incredible strength. Everywhere people argued lustily about the successor of Zhou, trying to figure out who would be the next Primier. I was eager to find out too, till one day Ge gave me a piece of paper. "This is Zhou's will," he told me. The will said Zhou wanted Deng Xiao-ping, who was the Vice Primier, to take his turn on duty. It wasn't any secret, since Deng was one of the possible successors, so I told my colleagues in the shop about the news and showed them the will. We all believed that Deng would be the Primier soon. Ge even thought his succession would make China more or less different, so he opened his chatter-box and told everybody his thoughts. He certainly never knew his chatter would draw him into a vortex of politics.

About two months after Zhao's death, Big Liu came to my house one night with a strained face.

"Bad news," he said as soon as he entered my room.

"Ge is locked in the headquarters," he said. He was very nervous.

"What's wrong?"

"Little Zhao said he's spread a political rumor about Zhou's will and Deng's succession. She said the Central Committee of the Party was very mad at the will. She said the will was a false will, and the police were looking for the will-maker all over the country. She said the will-maker was a counterrevolutionary."

"So what? Ge certainly isn't the will-maker."

"I know. They are trying to get him to tell who gave him the will, then following the vine to get the melon to track down the real maker."

"Did he tell?"

"I don't know."

"He could tell them he found the will himself somewhere in a bus, a touring boat, or a garden."

"They won't believe him. I'm afraid he will suffer for his silence."

"Do you think he will keep his chatter-box shut?"

"I'm not sure. But what if the will was given by his family, his best friend, or someone he doesn't want to put into trouble."

"Yes, I know."

I was worried about Ge when I was called by the Party

Secretary myself. There were three of them waiting for me in the office, the Party Secretary, Little Zhao and a member of the Party branch in our center.

"Sit down," the Party Secretary said. "Don't be nervous. We just want to ask you something."

I wasn't nervous at all because I knew what I was here for.

"I think you won't deny the fact that you have passed the will around in your shop?" he said.

"No."

"Who gave you the will?"

"Nobody. I found it on a seat of a bus. Somebody left it on purpose, I think."

"Don't lie to us, Li Ling," the member of the Party branch said. "Nobody will believe your nonsense."

"I've seen too much of your acting in the political study class," Little Zhao said. "Don't try to fool us anymore. You won't have your way this time if you refuse to make a clean breast of it."

Her words enraged me. I could never forget it was she and her organization who ruined my prospects with their political arms such as the political study class, the curse of bourgeois ideas and bourgeois world outlook. Now they tried to ruin Ge by the same means.

"Tell us the truth," the Party Secretary said. His face was turning blue. "Who gave you the will?"

"I already told you the truth," I said.

"But Ge Qiang said he gave you guys the will," Little Zhao said.

I didn't expect that she would mention Ge. "No, he didn't," I said.

"He's confessed already," the member of the Party branch said. "He said he gave you and several other people the will."

"I can't believe it," I said. "Because I did find the will on a bus. Maybe he mixed up my name with somebody else."

I could tell they were very mad. But I didn't care. They had no evidence, they couldn't do me any harm. At last, they asked me to write down what I had said and let me off.

I went to Big Liu's home, and met Bamboo Pole there. We found out we had the same fate that day.

"Did you tell them the truth?" Bamboo Pole asked me.

"No. I told them I found the will on a bus."

"Me too."

"Me too," Big Liu shouted. "The Party Secretary said how could you all find the will on the bus? It's certainly a lie."

We all laughed. But the laughter faded away when we remembered Ge was still locked up and nobody knew when it would end.

Ge came back to us when the will-maker had been found

somewhere in China. Needless to say, we were all happy to be together again. Ge hadn't changed any, although he had been locked up for almost three weeks and questioned almost every day. He opened his chatter-box and told us how he had been when he was locked in the center.

"I kept telling them I found the will on a bus," he said.

"Oh, my Lord!" I sighed, all three of us burst into laughter.

"Why?" Ge was confused.

"We all told them that we found the will on the bus! That certainly drove them crazy."

Ge laughed too. "But they told me you all confessed."

It was our small success because they couldn't punish Ge at last, although they would be willing to.

In the early fall of that year, the red sun was fallen. The whole nation sank into the deep grief at losing her supreme leader and the idol of the country. Anxiety about the future was everywhere in the country. I acted like a chatter-box too, asking everyone I met about what was going on in the Central Committee of the Party right now. I read newspaper every day and paid great attention to the political events. I couldn't help but guess who would be the winner and what would happen to China.

The downfall of the Gang of Four became the greatest event of the year. Everywhere in our country, from city to countryside, people toasted and celebrated. The liquor stores, the first time in their history, had sold out all kinds of wine within a day and had to call for emergency delivery. I was excited too, because I knew something was happening.

The situation changed as fast as people could dream and the future became brighter than ever. My father came back his position at the end of that year and my mother was busy again at her school. Hundreds and thousands urban youth left countryside for home and the door of our country was opened to the foreigners.

When spring came, both central and local newspapers carried the big news that the system of entrance exams for university would be resumed. It was the first time in ten years that our government put its hand to it with an administrative decree. From now on, the university would open its door to the public in spite of applicant's family and background.

It was great news for me. But I was still discouraged by my earlier failure and Little Zhao's threat.

"Don't worry about that," my father said. "The times have changed. Nobody can hold it back. I will go to school if necessary. They will understand that only happened in the preposterous time!" He now worked fine and was full of vitality. At our dinner table, the stories of his patient came out again.

"But they still have their powers in their hands."

"Nobody can go against government. They can't either. The only thing I worry about is if you can pass the exam. Because the university has been closed for ten years, there will be hundreds and thousands young people like you going to try their luck. It will be the hardest entrance exam than ever. In ten years, how many people have been wasted and suffered! You have to fight for your chance now."

11

Entering the university that year became the last chance to those who wanted to change jobs, who had been suffering, who were jobless and who loved to read and write since they were born. All of them had bet their dreams on passing the exams. So, it was very easy to imagine how hard the entrance exams would be. Only one out of twenty applicants would be accepted.

While I was busy reviewing, Liu passed the entrance exam of Shanghai Conservatory of Music and was waiting for the announcement in his country band. I was sure he would be the winner this time, although I wasn't sure about myself. I just couldn't stop worrying whether my opponents were stronger than I expected, or if the exam questions would be very, very difficult. To calm myself down, I could do nothing but study harder and harder. Every day, I got up at dawn and went to bed after midnight.

My colleagues in the shop all took a wait-and-see attitude except Chen, who encouraged me to fight for a chance. Because, as he said, a college graduate could have a better chance. "After we had supported commercial departments for years in the Great Leap Forward period, all college graduates were called back by the former companies. But us, who had no record of formal schooling, sank deeply into the bottom of the society. Clerks like us were always looked down on whether in the old society or the new society."

"Why didn't you fight for your fate?" Liang asked.

"I was almost thirty at that time. You are different, Li Ling. You are young and smart; you should do your best and try."

"I'm not sure if you could be accepted," Liang said. "But I would hate to see you leave."

"Me too," Chen said. "But you should try anyway."

I hated to leave them too. After all these years, we had been friends, although sometimes there would be a small brush between us.

The announcement took a long time to come, because it was the first time after ten years, and there were so much works to do. Moreover, the standard of admission should be carefully discussed and made. Anyway, it took a half a year more than usual process.

During this extra half year, I went to work every day and waited. Everyone who met me would ask if I knew the result.

"No, not yet," I kept answering.

Because I was the first and the only one who took the new entrance exam in the company, I became very popular. Every day, some people would come to me and ask me questions. Young men asked me, because they wanted to try the next time; the old men asked me because they wanted their kids to try. Even the girls who used to avoid seeing me two years ago came, one by one. They seemed to immediately forget what had I done to their sister Mary, and some of them even tried to ingratiate themselves with me. In their eyes, I might be already a quasi-graduate who would be the best choice of a marriage.

The day all schools started to send out the admission notices was Monday. I knew the news when I got up at noon and read the newspaper. I called Yan several times to check whether there was anything for me. When evening came, I couldn't help but think if I failed.

When I was going to leave for working next morning, I felt my heart jump incredibly fast. It should be the day I got the notice; otherwise, I failed.

Facing customers and working as usual were the most difficult things for me to do. I just couldn't concentrate. I waited and waited till afternoon when Yan cam back from the company and brought me a big yellow envelope on which I read the name of the school to which I had applied.

"It came yesterday," Yan said.

If I got it yesterday! But it didn't matter anymore. I got it at last, so I was satisfied.

"Congratulations," Liang said and Chen said and everyone said. The same as their wait-and-see attitude before, my acceptance didn't arouse them as much as I expected. They accepted the fact good-humoredly and calmly as if they knew what the result would be. But when I said goodbye to them in evening, Liang's eyes were wet and Chen shook hands with me for a long time.

"You won't be back," Liang said. "I know it."

I looked at her and she looked at me. I knew she was right. I wouldn't go back, ever. Maybe someday I would visit them, but I wouldn't go back.

The congratulations between my friends and I was much different. I spent my whole month's salary, 48 yuan (12 dollars at that time), to invite all of them to celebrate with me in a restaurant. We ordered several dishes and half dozen beers and ate and drank and talked and proposed toasts and had fun.

The following day I went to the center to transfer my personal credentials and I met Little Zhao in the office who had to write me a paper to testify my membership of CYL.

"Congratulations!" She smiled at me when she saw me in and shook hands with me. "I've known you'd have a splendid future; see, my point has been proved."

I said nothing. What could I say?

"Well, this is your paper. I wrote a letter to your school yesterday to certify to your honesty and good personality. We are very pleased to send you to the university and I wish you a good luck."

"Thank you," I took the paper and tried to leave.

"By the way, can I ask something if you have time?"

"What?"

"I want to ask if you can help my son. He's not good at math."

"How old is he?"

"Oh, he's only fifteen. But I hope he can enter the university when he graduates from high school. That will be the best way for him."

I looked at her. She looked at my supplicatingly, as if she had totally forgotten what had she done to me in last three years.

"Well, you know I should live in the campus during the week. I don't know if I will have time at weekend."

"But if you have time, can you promise me? I know you hate me . . . but it's not my fault. I was fooled too, like others."

"All right, I'll try," I said. When I finally freed myself from her, I felt like I had tasted a dead fly, vomited to death.

School opened in February 1978. It was a delayed opening as well as a new beginning. I left the place I had been working for five years and went into a new land where I would spend the next four years of my life.

Part Three

A Lilly In The Mirror

1

"Li Ling, why do your papers always get A's? Is Prof. Wang your uncle?" The speaker was Chen Andi who was the youngest in our dorm room.

"You spent too much time on girls, Andi," Wu said. He was thirty and a father of three kids. He came from countryside and was an old-fashioned, inflexible guy. "Otherwise, you would do a better job."

"I don't care if I can get A," Andi said. He started to take off his clothes. The lights were turned off every night at ten in campus so that we had to be back before ten. After washing, everyone went to bed and started to talk. The room I lived in was twenty feet long and fifteen feet wide. There were three bunk beds and a huge rectangular table on which all of us could do our homework and write letters. Andi and I were young, so we slept on the upper bunks, Wu was older so he slept under Andi. "Only your elders care."

"I care because I have less time than you guys," Wu said. "The Cultural Revolution wasted eleven years, the most valuable time in my life. If you were as old as I am when you entered university, you would care about everything."

"You are really lucky, Andi," Fu said. He was twenty-eight years old and the father of a one-year-old daughter. "You don't have to worry about anything when you study. But I have so many things to worry about. I have to worry about my wife, who is alone with a baby; about my daughter, who's only one and needs a father to stay with her; about the financial problems of my family—since my scholarship can hardly support myself, and my wife's salary isn't enough for the whole family."

"That's right, Andi," I said. I was six years older than Andi. "You are lucky because you have plenty of time."

"Lim is lucky too," Andi said. "He's only two years older than I am."

Lim was very shy, and he blushed easily. He slept over Four-eyes who came from our capital Peking and was the same age as Wu. "Don't count me, Andi," Lim said. "You are the only one in our room who has time to run after girls." He was interested in girls too, but he could never be as bold as Andi.

"You guys can all run after girls, but me," Four-eyes said. His real name was Jin Ron, but we all called him Four-eyes since he wore a pair of thick glasses. "My wife can smell if I want a girl, or even look at a girl."

We all laughed. He was a short man with a good sense of humor.

"But she's far away now," Andi said.

"Yes. But unfortunately, she said she could read from my letters if I was interested in any girl."

"My God!"

"What would she do if she knew you were interested in girls?" I asked.

"I can't tell, it's painful."

"Please! What would she do?" Andi asked.

"She would force me to make love with her ten times a day!" He said at last and sighed.

"Oh! Gosh!" Wu and Fu cried out in shock.

As the days passed, we lived happily. As a first year junior majoring in biology, I took six courses per semester, spending all the time in the classroom and lab. About ten minutes before ten, I went back dorm and chatted with my roommates. We gradually knew each other's romances as Fu's wife was his high school classmate. They got married when they were still in countryside. Four-eyes' wife was a worker in a factory. Lim used to have a girl-friend, but she left him when she found a richer man. Andi was a big boy who wanted to be in love all the time but never got the chance. I denied that I had fallen in love with any girl but they couldn't believe me. Four-eyes said it was unbelievable that a young man like me had never had a love affair. He thought I had had at least a half dozen girl-friends. So I finally confessed that I used to have a girl-friend when I was a teenager. I didn't dare to tell them about Mary.

"Now," Andi said when he heard my story. "I know why you are never interested in girls. You have a lover in your heart."

"You should forget her. She's only a dream, you know," Wu said seriously. "A dream is unrealistic, and you can't always wallow in a dream."

"I know."

One night, I went to the liberal arts reading room in main library, looking up some literary data. I was taking a Chinese course, a required course for all the students of science and engineering. I didn't know much about literary periods or events, although I loved to read novels and short stories. With the deadline of a term paper coming, I had to push the door of the reading room open and work on it.

I didn't see her till I took some books from bookstacks and went back to my seat. She was reading a book when I sat down, and I glanced at her occasionally. She was nearly my age, and her outward appearance told me that she didn't live in our town. When I tried to study, something familiar in her face drew my eyes to her involuntarily again.

She kept reading, though she certainly noticed my furtive glances at her. But she didn't even lift her eyes once. I knew it was impolite to stare, but I couldn't help it. Her coldness just increased my curiosity, because, as I always knew, girls never grudged their smiles to a man who was looking at them attentively. She was very uneasy, too, and couldn't even turn a single page over. That certainly meant something.

"Haven't we met before?" I asked uncertainly.

"Yes," she sighed and raised her head. I could hardly control my feelings when I saw her eyes. Could a dream come true? I stared at her dumbly. She seemed too far away for me to make me believe it was true.

"Fang-fang?" My voice quavered.

"Yes."

"Oh, my Lord! Is that true?"

"It's true. It's me." Her voice was unbelievably calm. "I knew you would find me someday."

"Tell me, are you a student here?"

"Hush!"

"Let's go outside."

I followed her outside. Then she told me she was a freshman of Chinese literature, and she lived in the dorm not far from my building.

"Why haven't I seen you before! We are only one building apart."

"I didn't want to disturb you, Li Ling."

"What? Disturb me? Why?" I told her eagerly how I had missed her these years and how my friends tried to persuade me to forget her. "They said it was a dream, but my grandma told me sometimes a dream comes true. See, she's right, my dream did come true."

"I think your friends are right," she said. "The past is already past. You and I now belong to the different societies and we live in different places. We are totally different from when we were teenagers."

"So what? I can't see any difference. Now you are back, and we are still friends."

She said nothing but turned her eyes to other direction.

"Tell me, Fang-fang, where do you live now?"

"I told you I live in the dorm."

"I mean where do you live in Shanghai? You certainly don't live where you used to."

She shook her head.

"So where?"

"We still live in Anhui."

"You mean you have been living with your parents in Anhui for eight years?"

"Yes. But my father was died a long time ago."

"I'm sorry."

So she had been living in Anhui. I should have realized how mush she had suffered when I saw her. Look at her rough skin that used to be tender and milky white; look at her wrinkly face that used to be pink and sweet; look at her withered hair that used to be black and bright. She wasn't a slim, fragile and lovely girl anymore, but a full-grown, rough and sturdy young woman. The only thing that didn't change on her was that dimples which appeared whenever she smiled.

"Then what do you do on weekends?"

"The same as weekdays."

"You can't always read and write," I said. "You need some break. Would you like to go to my house this weekend? My parents would love to see you."

"No, I can't. I will visit your parents someday, but not now."

Her indifference was deliberate, intentional. Maybe we had been separated too long.

"Do you remember the tiny flower you gave to me? I still keep it in my book. I look at it every day as if looking at you."

I saw her eyes sparkling when I mentioned the flower, but the light died immediately.

We said goodbye before ten. I asked her to go with me to the library the following night. She refused. She said she had an appointment with her professor. "He's my father's friend, you know."

"What about the day after tomorrow?"

"No, you should work alone," she smiled.

I blushed. I knew I wouldn't concentrate if she was there. "Then, when can we see each other again?"

"We will have time. It's only the second semester, right?"

So we said goodbye at last. She didn't even let me shake her hand but waved a farewell.

Although the meeting wasn't romantic at all, it still brought me the greatest happiness. Fang-fang was alive, and better than that, she was my school-mate.

I ran to the dorm as happy as a child. I couldn't even wait to put down my notebook to tell my roommates that I had found the lover of my childhood.

"Where is she?" Andi asked, full of curiosity.

"Here! On campus! She's a student in Chinese Department. Her father used to work there."

"Is she still beautiful?" Four-eyes asked.

"Oh, yes. She's always beautiful."

"She's certainly changed a lot," Wu said.

"Yes. She had been working in Anhui for eight years."

"What a pity!" Fu said. "She isn't a tender pink princess anymore."

"Yes," I said dejectedly. "She was quite indifferent to me too."

"Why?" Lim asked. "Did she still love you?"

"Maybe she just wasn't sure what to do," Andi said. "You have been separated for eight years!"

"Maybe she's married," Wu said.

"Oh, no!" I cried. "I think it was a young woman's reserved manner. We aren't teenagers anymore."

"Anyway, you will find out soon."

I didn't see her the next day, even the whole next week. More than once, I tried the enter the humanities building to look for her when I passed by. I gave up only because I was afraid it would bother her. I regretted terribly that I forgot to ask her room number, otherwise, I could visit her when I had the chance.

That weekend, I was too impatient to wait for Liu's call but ran to him and told him the story.

"Oh, we should have a reunion party," Liu said joyfully. He lighted up with surprise and pleasure when he heard the news. "Maybe we should go to the Old Market again."

"Good idea. But I'm not sure if she will accept the invitation."

"Where is your self-confidence, guy? Keep trying. You can't expect a sedate young lady to show you her real feeling at the first time she sees you after eight years separation."

"I don't know her room number," I said. "I'm not sure I can find her in the campus. You are the initiator. She certainly won't refuse you."

"All right, all right. I'll do it. I'll write her a letter, invite her to go with us the next weekend."

I couldn't wait till the next weekend. Every day during the week I went to class ten minutes early to pace up and down around the humanities building, or went into the reading room in the evening. But I couldn't find her. She seemed to be hiding somewhere on the campus. I was afraid that she was trying to avoid me, but I couldn't think of any reason why she would do that. Till the weekend when I came back home on Saturday and read her letter at Liu's house, I was freed from worry at last. She said she was glad to accept our invitation and would go with us to the market, which she called a favorite place of her childhood.

"See," Liu said triumphantly. "I told you she would come, didn't I?"

Sunday morning I got up early and carefully shaved. I called on Liu as soon as I finished and urged him unceasingly to hurry.

"Oh, poor Li Ling, you're crazy."

We arrived the market half an hour earlier than the arranged time. The Sunday market was always crowded. People were coming in and out while we were waiting.

"I hope she won't be late," I said. We had been raising our

117

heads and standing on tiptoes for a long time. Liu was looking forward to meeting her too.

She arrived just on time. "The traffic is terrible," she said apologetically when she knew we had been waiting for her for half an hour. "I almost forgot what the Shanghai traffic looked like."

"I hope you didn't forget the labyrinth in the Old Market," Liu said.

"Yes, I do forget," she smiled.

"Oh, my God! I don't want to be lost in the market like a little kid!"

She laughed. All at once, we seemed to be back in the sixties while we were all teenagers. "You won't," she said. "Li Ling should help. He's a typical Shanghainese." She looked at me. From her smiling eyes, I saw the familiar insight.

"All right, just follow me."

The labyrinth in the Old Market consisted of numerous narrow winding trails, with hundreds stores and shops. Instead of the colorful revolutionary slogans of the past, there were advertisements and pictures on the walls. The temple of city gods was reopened. It was a shopping mall now.

"Do you remember the monkey show?" We were passing the open ground in front of the temple.

"Oh, absolutely," she said.

"I remember the first time when you saw the snake man, you were almost too scared to look at him," Liu said.

"Did I? I can't remember that," she said with a red face.

We entered the famous garden Yu Yuan, visited the toy stores, and followed the old tracks.

"I could never imagine being back here again with you guys," she said.

"That kind of thinking was a luxury when all you had for company were the buffalos and the oil lamp," Liu said.

"Yes," she said shortly.

She didn't talk about her past, and we didn't ask. But from what she did say, I was sure she at least had the same experiences as Liu.

"Nanqiang meat-filled tiny buns!" Liu cried like a child. "My favorite."

"I almost forgot what it tastes like," she said. When we were kids, the tiny buns were her favorite too.

"Let's go. Li Ling will pay for it. He's the richest man in the world."

"Why?" she laughed.

"I had been working for five years before I entered school, so I can bring my salary with me."

"It's not fair, you know. I have been in countryside for seven years, but I couldn't get anything."

"The problem is, I'm supported by my old unit, and no place could support you."

"Yes, I know. But it's just unfair, right?"

"Yes, I agree," she said.

"Unfortunately, there is too much unfairness in the world," I said.

"For that reason, you should pay for everything we eat today."

"You got it."

Fang-fang laughed again when she saw us making the deal seriously.

I couldn't have asked for a more harmonious atmosphere as we talked, walked and ate. When I saw Fang-fang and Liu keep working on the table and crying that they couldn't eat anymore, I couldn't help but laugh and laugh.

"We should come here every month," Liu said when we left market for home.

"Oh, yes," she said.

"Do you agree?"

"Jesus! How can I agree? I'll drop half my salary here."

They laughed, and we laughed, and everybody looking at us laughed.

"I had a wonderful weekend," she said when we said goodbye at the bus-station. She had the most charming smile, "Thank you, both of you."

"See you next time," Liu said. "I'll arrange another party for you soon, and Li Ling will pay for it."

"Oh, poor Li Ling," she laughed again.

"See," Liu patted my shoulder happily. "I told you she was the same girl we knew. I'm glad she's back with us."

"Me too."

"Now, you should take the second step all by yourself. Good luck!" He grinned at me as he waved a farewell in front of my house.

2

Andi told us the Chinese Department was holding a dance next Friday in Students Hall.

"Really?" Four-eyes asked with great interest.

Dancing was very popular before the Revolution. My father had told me when he was a college student, he went every week. But it had been swept away as a dirty bourgeois thing during the Revolution. So Andi, Lim and I had never had the chance to go dancing before. Wu grew up in the countryside. He was as ignorant as any of us, although he was one of the oldest in our class. Fu knew a little bit about dance because he used to see people dance when he was a teenager. But Four-eyes said he was familiar with the waltz, tango, and other names I had never heard of.

"Yes. One of my fellow provincials told me tonight." Andi liked to get acquainted with his fellow provincials on campus, so he had his provincial friends all over the school.

"Did they invite us?" Fu asked.

"I don't know. But we can go and take a look."

"If you want, you can join in on your own initiative," Four-eyes said.

"Yes, I will," Fu said. At the same time, Four-eyes had already taken a pillow and started to dance.

"Oh," Andi stared at him. "Can you teach me? I would like to go to the dance party too."

"That's easy. Follow me. One, two, three; one, two, three . . ."

It was a funny scene when two of them holding pillows in their arms, dancing lightly in a tiny space. But nobody laughed at them. We all looked at them with the utmost concentration.

While they were dancing and we were watching with keen interest, the lights were turned off. The room was immediately full of sighs.

"All right, I'll teach you tomorrow," Four-eyes comforted Andi, who had been sighing in deep despair.

"Great! When?"

"Half past nine in the evening."

To my surprise, all of us were back our dorm before that time the following day, including Wu, who usually was the last one home.

Four-eyes made no secret of his triumph. He had us move the table aside and take a pillow each. But Wu refused to do it, he said he only wanted to watch.

"Come on," Four-eyes said. "If you only want to watch, why don't you wait till next week?"

"It's the best chance to make friends with girls, Wu. Don't blow it," Andi said.

But he couldn't be persuaded. At last, all of us danced clumsily behind Four-eyes except Wu, who sat on his bed and watched us.

A week was a very short time for us new learners. With the day fast approaching, we tried to practice everywhere possible, even in the bathroom. Andi was almost lost in dance. He hummed the dancing music anytime and walking as though he was dancing with a rolling gait everywhere. Lim was shy, but he practiced in our room whenever we were out. He came back earlier and danced behind the door.

Wu was an ardent audience, although he never tried to learn himself. Once when we pooled our efforts to push him to dance, he even blushed. Fu was the quickest learner, and he could dance gracefully after several practices. I couldn't dance as well as Four-eyes and Fu, but better than Andi and Lim, I thought. Dancing to me not only meant an amusement, or a new excitement, but also a hope. From the first day I heard the news, I had made up my mind that I would go to the ball. It was held by Chinese Department, and Fang-fang would be there. I wouldn't abandon any chance of seeing her again. If I was lucky, I would even get a chance to dance with her.

We all went to dance Friday night. The Students Hall was full when we arrived. In the center of the hall, there were already three or four couples dancing to the music. Obviously, there were many more watchers than the dancers. Even the Chinese Department, most of the students were hesitant to move forward. I was looking for Fang-fang, while Andi and Four-eyes were ready to try.

"You certainly dance better than they do," Fu told Andi who was as impatient as a monkey. "Go, show them something."

All the young dancers on the dance floor were half unskilled and half in a muddle. Some of them even couldn't follow the beat of the music. But they were brave men anyway.

Andi joined in the second turn. He invited a girl in front of him. We all laughed when he held the girl stiffly, making the small, intense circles.

"Lim, come with me," Four-eyes said to Lim.

"No, you first," Lim shrank back and hid behind me.

"Li Ling, what about you?"

"I'll wait for a while," I said. I hadn't seen Fang-fang yet. Also, I was afraid to be the object of all the eyes here.

"Maybe I should go with you," Fu said. "Otherwise, all the time I spent learning is a waste."

121

"That's the point!" Four-eyes said. "Come on, Li Ling, Lim, and all of you!"

He and Fu went when the music started again. Four-eyes immediately became the center of people's attention. I could see the admiration in the girls' eyes and even in the men's.

"Our room will be in the limelight tonight," said Wu, who had been standing beside me.

"Maybe we should go next turn," I said.

"Not me," he said. "I'll be the loyal audience."

"I'll follow you if you go," Lim said.

"Shall we try?"

We did it at last, casting all caution to the winds. I invited a girl I had seen and Zhang invited a girl in our class. His face was brighter when he brought the girl out to dance. Now, everyone in our room, except Wu, were dancing on the floor.

It was a waltz. While I followed the music, making small circles around the center, I kept looking for Fang-fang. I knew she was certainly somewhere in the audience. Suddenly, I met the eyes I was so familiar with in the corner. She was there! I couldn't dance anymore, with an unlovely girl!

The music was inconceivably long. My dancing partner kept stepping on my feet since she had never danced before. When the music finally ended at long last, I felt like a prisoner released from the jail.

She saw me too when I was dancing. She blushed like a little girl when I forced my way over to her, and invited her to dance with me. "Oh, I can't," she said.

"Please!"

"I can't dance, you know."

"It doesn't matter, just follow me. Please."

She let herself go with me, as shy as a baby. As soon as my hand touched her waist, she started to dance beautifully.

"How can you be a dancer!" she cried when we were following the music, revolving around.

"My roommate taught me," I said. I told her about how we practiced in our room, holding a pillow.

She laughed when she heard the story, and her face immediately became a blooming flower. I looked at her like an idiot.

She lowered her beautiful eyes and said, "Please don't look at me like that."

"You are so beautiful, Fang-fang," I couldn't help saying that.

She was flushed. For a long time, we had been looking at each other silently. The music stopped, then changed into another. We danced, and simply danced.

"I love you," I told her at last.

She said nothing but held me closer. I felt her hair touch

mine, and her breath was warming my face from time to time. I was excited. My heart was burning, and I was short of breath.

"Let's out of here," I said and brought her through the crowded hall into a open ground outside. As soon as we were away from the crowd, we held each other and kissed.

"Oh, my love," I murmured when I kissed her and stroked her.

She started to tremble when my hand touched her body. "Oh, please, please stop," she cried helplessly.

But I couldn't stop. My hands were on her back and I tried to unbutton her. "Oh, no!" She pushed me away hardly when I started to kiss her bare breasts. "We can't do it here!"

I stopped. I felt some irritation in her voice.

"I'm sorry," I was very depressed.

"It's not your fault," she said softly. "I love you too, but we can't indulge in it too much. We should learn to control ourselves."

"Why?" I was confused in her unimaginable calmness. How could she become so cool after all of that had happened between us?

"Because we are in school, and we can't let it destroy our peaceful life."

"But we aren't ascetics, are we? The school life and love are not contradictory."

"But love not only means making love," she seemed to be insulted.

"I'm sorry. I didn't mean that."

"All right. From now on, we could only be friends, maybe good friends."

"But you will see me sometimes during the week?"

"Yes."

"Then I agree."

We kissed again, without passion. "Ok, it's the time for bed," she said. We walked quietly to the dorm.

"Bye," she smiled at me when we were separated in front of her building.

"Bye, I love you."

I was back to my room just in time. When the lights were turned off, I was already in my bed.

"Ah, Li Ling, we thought you would be the last," Fu said when he came with others in the darkness. "But you are the first."

"I saw your girl-friend at the ball," Andi said. "She's older than you, right?"

"But she's pretty," Four-eyes said. "A very charming girl."

"Oh, yes. She is."

But I didn't want them to judge Fang-fang as if she was a model. So I interrupted them and asked, "Lim, I saw you keep

123

dancing with the same girl all the time."

"Oh, yes," Andi said. "He's crazy about her."

"Don't be a blabbermouth, Andi," Wu said. "You are the same."

"Tell us, who is your girl?" Fu asked.

"She is the student in the English Department, and she is two years older than me."

"See, he already knows her age!" Lim tried to hit him back.

"In the western world, young men marrying older women is a fashion," Four-eyes said.

"But my folks are old-fashioned, they won't accept an older daughter-in-law."

"Come on, you aren't an old bloke, are you?" Four-eyes said.

"Anyway, you will be punished soon," Andi said back. "If your wife knows that you have been dancing with a hundred girls a night."

"I won't tell, you know."

When we all lay on our beds, Andi said, "That kind of dance should be held more often."

"Yes," Zhang said. "At least once a week."

"I will try next time I think," Wu said. "I can't have all you guys are in the limelight without me."

We laughed and claimed that he certainly would surpass everyone in the room if he went to the dance.

3

The campus became lively and noisy again when our second school year started in the fall. The first day's reunion was exciting. After two months of summer vacation, we had lots to tell and lots to eat. Wu brought us a huge bag of his Shandong fresh jujubes, big and red; Four-eyes brought us different kind of Peking dry fruit as well as other special local products; Andi brought us five pounds of Shanxi roast peanuts, and Lim brought us his hometown specialty: honey pears. We sat around the table in our room, talking and eating.

I told them eagerly about the trip to the Yellow Mountain with my friends Ge, Big Liu and Bamboo in August; and how splendid the landscape was, how vivid the shaped stones were and how happy we were. Fu had been staying with his family the whole vacation so that he could tell us nothing but how cute his daughter was and how happy his wife was.

Four-eyes had traveled with his wife to Qingdao, the beautiful seacoast city in the north, and had climbed up the Taishan, one of the five famous mountains, on their way home. He eagerly described how comfortable to be strolling around the seashore and sandy beach during the summer, and how grand and magnificent the Taishan Mountain was, with its numerous stories and legends.

Lim's home wasn't far from the sea, so he went almost every day to swim.

"So," Andi said. "You're as dark as an Indian."

We all laughed and urged Wu to tell us his story.

"No," he shook his head. "I have nothing to tell."

"I can't believe it," Andi said. "Sixty days together with your wife and three kids! You certainly have something to tell."

"Yes, after one year's separation, the summer vacation should be another honeymoon to you," Four-eyes said.

"Don't tease me," Wu seemed mad. "I'm not as lucky as you."

"Did you have fun, at least?" Lim asked.

"No."

"How come!" Andi cried. "Everyone had fun, but you!"

"I'm going to tell you a story, anyway." Wu said after he had made up his mind. "Because I don't want you guys to misunderstand if somedays something should happen to me."

"All right, all right, please tell!" We all looked at him while he started to tell us his story.

"It was a long story anyhow," he said. "I grew up in a poor but *black* family. Because my grandfather was a landlord, we went down to the bottom of the society right after 1949. My father is a middle school teacher who has been struggling all his life, since he is a son of a landlord. Every month, his sixty-yuan salary had to support the whole family: his parents who lost their property in 1949; his wife and two sons. I am the elder son and my younger brother died from hunger in the 1960's. I was dying too when my father finally dashed in and brought me two steaming breads. Before my grandfather died, his last wish was having a chicken wing. But at that time, we didn't even have a single feather of chicken at home!

"I loved to read and write since I was a high school student, but I still couldn't escape the fate of being sent back to the farm. I kept writing, and finally published some articles in the local newspapers. At that time, I wanted nothing but to leave the farm someday. Some of the units in our county had tried to hire me when they saw my articles, but they all backedaway when they learned my family background. I was not strong when I was young because of malnutrition. I couldn't earn as much as others at the farm. So ten years ago, when my mother was fatally ill, my family started to look for a woman for me because my family needed her to take care of and support.

"I had fought against it, but shamefully failed, because I couldn't solve the problem of my family's needs. The night of our wedding, I cried alone in my room, then came out to see my bride. She was a strong woman, five years older than I am. She lived with us in the same village, and I knew her when I was a little boy. Because she had had smallpox, she had hard time finding a boy-friend when she grew up. Her parents were eager to find her a husband, so that they didn't nitpick too much about my family background. And she became my wife when I was twenty.

"During the Cultural Revolution, we could do nothing but bear children. We never talked when we were alone. Every night, she laid herself down barely beside me, waiting for me. I'm not sure if she loves it or hates it, because she never told me. Maybe she thinks it's just a thing that men and women do. Sometimes I couldn't stand her silent indifference and left her alone on the bed. But she never complained. She would do the same thing the following day till I was stirred again by her body.

"After ten years, we had had three kids and she became the pillar of our family. If the situation hadn't changed, and if I hadn't had the chance to go back to school, we might well be living like this forever. But after living with you guys for a year, I hopelessly found out that I can't stand her anymore; because we don't love each, and we never did. The only thing that ties us together is the responsibility of our family."

126

"Maybe you should divorce," Andi said.

"I don't know," Wu said. "I have tried to make up my mind, but I can't. We have three kids, and she has done so much for my family."

The whole room was quiet when he lifted his eyes and looked at us. What could we say? We could neither tell him he should divorce nor persuaded him to keep the marriage. But I would support him if he wanted to be divorced.

I saw Fang-fang again in front of her building that evening. I had been waiting for her since I had had supper.

"Li Ling, so nice to see you again," she said happily when she saw me and gave me both her hands. "What about the trip to the Yellow Mountain? Did you enjoy it?" I had invited her to go with me, but she refused. She said she had to visit her lonely mother in Anhui.

"Oh, yes," I said. "How about you? Did you enjoy the life at home?"

"Yes," she smiled. "I told my mother you are here. She said hello to you. She still remembers you."

"I will visit her next summer," I said. "If you allow."

"Why not?" She said unwillingly.

"That will be great. We can climb up the Yellow Mountain again. It's so beautiful! You should see it."

Her smile faded and she started to move ahead.

"Shall we go somewhere tonight? I want to show you a secret place."

"What secret place?"

"Follow me, I found it the first day when I entered the school."

It was not too far from the main sports yard, a hill with luxuriant grasses and trees. It was the border of the campus, and people hardly came in the evenings, especially the first night of the school year.

"It's so quiet," she said when we sat down on the ground.

"A quiet place, a beautiful night, and only you and I to share it." I sat beside her and kissed her. She leaned against me and enjoyed the kissing. "I miss you, Li Ling," she said.

"I love you," I murmured. I had been stirred but I couldn't do anything more because I still remembered what she said to me outside the dance hall.

She put her arms around my neck when I kissed her. Her body was like a fire burning my consciousness little by little. I cried painfully when I found that I couldn't control myself anymore. I believed I would die if she refused me and stood up right now. But she didn't. Her response to my crazy touching was clinging to me and kissing me.

I was too impatient to unbutton her but moved under her skirt and looked for the place I should enter. I was a virgin

127

indeed although I had tried once with Mary. No matter how hard I worked, I still couldn't get myself in. I started to moan with the fire of thirst and pain. My hands rubbed her breasts. She cried as she took my stiff penis in her hand. I felt a burst of sensation touch the depths of my soul as she guided me into her body. I worked and moved and felt I was absolutely melted into her.

When consciousness came back at long last, I found her sitting beside me, stroking my hair.

"Fang-fang?" I called her name uncertainly.

"Yes?" She looked at me with the most beautiful smile which made me immediately jump at her and kissed her again.

"Oh, no," she laughed and ran away.

"I love you," I shouted at her with deep love and pleasure. She ran back to me and we embraced each other.

Under the dim moonlight, we walked slowly towards our dorm at midnight. It was so quiet in the darkness that shrouded around the campus. We walked arm in arm quietly, as if a part of the darkness. I was so happy; and I could feel nothing but her.

"Love you, sweetheart," I said when we said goodbye in front of her dorm building.

"Bye," she kissed me and disappeared in the door.

I was back when all my roommates had fallen into deep sleep. I lay on my bed without washing and immediately sank into dreamland.

4

Dance became a regular Friday night program on our campus. Shortly after dinner on Friday, everybody in our room was busy changing and washing. Andi and Lim were dance fiends who went dance every week and stayed from very beginning till the end. I thought dance was a good entertainment to enliven my boring life of study and a good chance to meet with Fang-fang. Fu and Four-eyes were somewhat like me, they liked to dance but weren't as crazy as the young boys.

Wu was very fond of dancing now. He made up his mind to divorce his wife after he had seen Fang-fang and me kissing goodbye in front of the dorm building.

"I never imagined love between man and woman could be so touching," he said one night when he came back from the library.

"What happened?" Andi asked.

"Nothing. I only saw Li Ling and his girl waving goodbye in front of the building tonight."

I was very embarrassed when I heard that he had seen us, but the rest of them asked Wu curiously about what he saw.

"I can't describe," he said. "You know, in our village, even a married couple could never walk hand in hand. Maybe you guys will laugh at me if I tell you the truth. My wife and I never kiss, although we already have three kids."

"What?" Andi jumped up on the bed and cried. "How can you make love without kissing?"

"That's nothing to be surprised at," Fu said. "The place I have settled down in is the same. I've never seen a man and woman walking hand in hand in the village, even in the small town. If they should walk together, the man walks at least ten feet apart from his wife, who always drags behind."

"It's very normal that the married couples never kiss in the countryside," Four-eyes said. "Once when I was in the suburbs of Peking, the village had a movie show. It was a love story. When and man and a woman were kissing in a scene, one of the married men asked, "What are they doing, mouth to mouth?""

"Oh, really?" Andi could only sigh.

"Don't forget we are the most conservative nation in the world. We have a five-thousand-year-old history and a billion old traditions and thoughts."

"That's why I was afraid to make the decision," Wu said. "but now I've made up my mind. I will divorce, because I want to love and be loved."

"Yes, that's the point," Four-eyes said. "We can't live without love."

Although we all agreed with what Wu had said, we knew clearly it would be very, very difficult for him to do because our government never encouraged people to be divorced. It was normal for a lawsuit of divorce kept to drag on for years; the longest record was thirty years. Some of the couples lived separated all their lives but never got divorced. Maybe it would be a little easier now, but none of us could assure him.

Days passed, then weeks passed. Liu invited Fang-fang and me to attend a school recital on New Year Eve. He was now crazy about a girl named Apple who was a pianist in his school.

"Apple will be my piano accompanist."

"Oh, really?"

Fang-fang and I attended the recital. There was a carnival party in our school too, but we wanted to spend the last night of the year with our friend Liu; and we were eager to see what Apple looked like.

When Liu came on stage, we pricked our ears and opened our eyes wide. Liu's playing was perfect. He had made great advances since he entered the school. Apple the girl we couldn't see clearly till she stood up from the piano and responded to the curtain call. That was a great-looking girl! When she played a piano solo after Liu, we got lost in her consummate artistry.

"She is great!" I told him when we met outside the hall after the recital was over.

"Yes. She's perfect," he said.

"Good luck, guy. I would like to meet your girl-friend."

"I'm working on it," he smiled.

I didn't go back home that night because Fang-fang had to go back school. It was late. We hardly saw anybody on our way because all the people were home for their New Year's Eve reunion parties. I put my arm around Fang-fang's shoulder so that we could be a little bit warmer.

"How could you imagine Liu would be a violinist when you saw him being forced to practice all the time?" she said.

"It's because of the Cultural Revolution," I said.

"Why?"

"That's a long story," I said. I told her how he left home for countryside when he graduated from high school, and how he was absolutely disappointed after he had been stuck there for years, and how he turned back to his violin and music seeking comfort. "He told me it was the violin that helped him to pass the most difficult time in the countryside."

"Yes, if I only had a violin!" She sighed.

I turned my eyes to her. Under the dim streetlights, her face was twisted with pain. "You've suffered a lot, I know."

She started to tremble when she looked at me. I stopped walking and held her into my arms. "Poor baby, please tell me, I can make you feel better." I kissed her tenderly.

"It's a nightmare," she said. "I can't even think of it now."

"Tell me what happened?"

Her eyes looked into mine. "Do you really want to know?"

"Yes."

She lowered her eyes and started to tell.

"You certainly remembered the day when we left Shanghai for Anhui where they said my father could get a job at the school. We arrived Anhui after we had spent two days on the train and the long-distance bus. But the place waiting for my father wasn't the classroom but the cowshed where he was locked up again. We knew later it was because they got the information from Shanghai and knew the newcomer was an escaped counterrevolutionary. My father certainly knew what it was so he hanged himself in the cowshed one night when the watcher was asleep.

"We knew of his suicide three days later, when somebody from school came and drove us away from the dorm building where we had been living since we arrived. They only told us my father had committed suicide and they would not let us go to say goodbye to his body. They said he had already been buried. So even now, we don't know exactly whether my father was killed or committed suicide because we haven't seen his body or his grave. Anyway, he's gone.

"We couldn't live at the school anymore, because my father was dead, and we couldn't be back Shanghai either. Driven by the Red Rebels, we left for a small village not far from the university and settled down.

"By day, we worked in the fields as farmers; in the evening, we stayed in a ruined temple that used to be the place villagers arranged for their dead people. We could barely support ourselves, although we did our best to struggle for survival. It was nine years ago, and I was sixteen.

"We suffered and suffered till one day I couldn't get up anymore. I was totally worn down by daily exceedingly hard work and extreme malnutrition. When I was dying on the ground of the ruined temple, one of our neighbors came and helped my mother to move me into his house. Since then, we lived with his family till the Cultural Revolution was over. I recovered gradually under his wife and children's meticulous care, and could stand up again three months later. They knew I loved to read, every time they went to the market, they would buy me some books, although the old couple couldn't read themselves. After seven years of living together, we are actually a family."

"Where is your mother now?" I asked. "What is she doing?"

"She's working at the university where my father spent the

131

last days of his life. She lives in the teacher's apartment at school."

The wind of winter night in Shanghai could go through to your bones. But we had been holding each other for a long time in the chilly wind. Although I knew she would have been suffering during those eight years, I was still shocked when I heard the story. She had been living like a forsaken dog before the kind-hearted family took them in. Oh, poor Fang-fang!

"It's already past," I said after drying her tears. "We won't let it happen to you again."

"I'm not sure about that," she said. "My suffering was only a part of our nation's. If the Cultural Revolution comes back, it could happen again."

"If the Revolution comes back, we can leave for abroad."

"How can we?"

"We can ask my grandparents for help. The Revolution was too miserable to suffer twice."

She forced a smile and said. "We'll see. Now we can only wish it won't ever happen again."

It was too late to have any bus on the street now. "What a pity," I said when I looked at the schedule at bus-stop. "We have to walk three miles to our school tonight."

"It doesn't matter," she said. "We can enjoy the quiet and peacefulness of the night."

"Okay, let's go."

"It would be so nice if we could take a walk every day," she said as we walked down the street hand in hand.

"We can do it every weekend if you like," I said. "Later on, when we graduate and get married, we can do it every day."

"No. We could never get married," she said. "When we graduate, I have to go back Anhui and you will stay in Shanghai."

"No. I will marry you and we will go to Anhui together. I won't let you leave again. Never."

"Don't be childish, Li Ling," she said. "You have to stay with your parents and take care of them. You can't leave them alone."

"They can move to Anhui and we can live together with them," I said. I knew there was no possibility she could move to our city, because Shanghai was too crowded already.

"No," she said stubbornly. "It's unrealistic."

"All right," I said. "We can still get married if we live separately."

"That's unrealistic too. It's very hard to keep the marriage if we live separately. We have to say goodbye when we graduate."

I could never know why she became so stubborn every time when I mentioned a marriage. She seemed too sober-minded. But I hoped she would change her mind when time passed. We had enough time to deal with that.

132

5

The winter vacation lasted almost three weeks. Compared with two-months summer vacation, it was too short for most of students to travel home.

In our room, only Four-eyes, who had enough money to support himself, and Wu, who had to go to court with his wife during the vacation; were leaving. Both Andi and Lim would stay on campus. As the local hosts, Fu and I invited them to be our special guests for Chinese New Year.

My parents were very happy to know that Fang-fang would spend three weeks with us. They had known her since she was a teenager. When I told them how much had she suffered in last eight years, they felt so bad, especially my father. He couldn't accept the fact that his patient was killed at last after he had cured him. They started to prepare for her coming as soon as we entered the final exams. They moved all my stuff into the sitting-room and made everything in my room fresh and clean for her. They had me sleep on the sofabed in the sitting-room and let her have my room. I would rather have stayed with her than slept separately, but it was impossible. My parents weren't old-fashioned, but very traditional. They wouldn't appreciate it if their son lived with a girl overtly at their home.

I remember clearly the day she moved into my home. It was the first day of the winter vacation, I picked her up at school and helped her carry her daily necessities. My mother took half a day off, shopping and cooking for us. On the dinner table, there were all delicious and sumptuous dishes we could only have in holidays. My father for the first time didn't tell us the story about his patients but talked to her.

"She's such a sweet girl," my mother said after she sent Fang-fang to her room. "Fate was too cruel to her."

"But we could make her happy now," my father said. "I could be her father if she likes."

"No, you should be her father-in-law," I corrected him. "I will marry her after we graduate and get jobs."

"Oh!" they still got surprised although they should have known my feelings.

"So you brought her home on purpose, my son," my father said.

"Yes," I laughed. "Anyway, I hope you like her."

"We all like her," my mother said.

"Yes, we do."

"Oh, thank you," I said and gave both of them a big hug.

The next morning, I was impatient for my parents to leave, and went into her room as soon as they locked the door behind them. She was still on her bed, waiting for me.

"I knew you would come," she said, and stretched out her arms to me.

"I'm as hungry as a wolf," I threw myself into her arms and kissed her. "I can't even wait."

Under a heavy quilt, she was wearing only a night dress and her breasts were almost naked. I gasped with admiration at her beautiful curves of body and soft skin, then became a captive of lust. I did it impatiently and she followed me passionately. Her body was a paragon of ripeness, soft, chubby, and springy. It was different from Mary's. Mary's breasts were chubby too, but sturdy as well; her breasts were as tender and soft as pads of cotton. A body like Mary's would stir a man's primitive passion, but a body like Fang-fang's would make a man get drunk.

It was wonderful when we were together. Every morning, I would go to her when my parents left. Sometimes we spent half the day on bed, making love or just lying together quietly and happily.

Right before the Chinese New Year, Liu had asked us to go for an outing with him. He had invited Apple and persuaded us to go with them. "Why?" I said. "It will be best for you if you are dating with her alone. How romantic, you walking with her, hand in hand, eyes to eyes, on the narrow country path! We don't want to be your mirrors or lights. No."

"Yes, I know," he said. "But she won't go with me alone. She accepted the invitation only when I told her we would go together with you."

"Don't make Liu feel bad," Fang-fang said. "It would be fun to hike in the country."

"So you accept it?" Liu lit up immediately. "I know you will. Thank you."

"Poor Liu," Fang-fang said when he left. "He's lost already. I hope that girl doesn't let him down."

"I got lost too," I said. "Will you let me down?"

She suddenly blushed and kissed me with all her might. I was melted in her erupting passion and started to work untiringly with her.

Apple was very charming. She was quiet, but she had a good sense of humor as well. We went together to the public park and a quaint garden in Jiading county of Shanghai, which had few visitors because of the cold weather. As soon as they met, the two girls became very close, leaving Liu and me behind as they walked and talked happily in front of us.

"See," Liu said. "She can talk to anybody like that but me."

"It's because there are four of us," I said. "If only two of you were here, she certainly would talk to you."

"She never will," he said. "She only talks to me when I ask her something."

"So," I shrugged my shoulders. "Maybe you need to ask her more often."

However, it became a turning point of their relationship.

"Apple came to me last night and asked me about the past," Liu told us the following day. "She said Fang-fang had told her that we used to be a band and I was the leader during the Cultural Revolution. And she wanted to know all the details. So I told her about the adventure in the hospital and some funny things in our childhood. When she heard about all I did to avoid playing the violin, she laughed as a child and told me she used to do the same thing when she was a kid. In the sound of our laughing, the distance between us suddenly became shorter. So finally I told her that I love her and . . . and . . ."

"And what?"

He blushed and started to hem and haw. "She lowered her head, so I went to her and . . . and kissed her." When he saw us burst out laughing, he added embarrassedly, "It's my first kiss, I mean, kiss a girl."

I knew, but I just couldn't help laughing. Even now, every time when I think of it, I still can't help laughing.

"Don't be upset," Fang-fang said while I was still laughing. "We aren't laughing at you."

"I know. I'm too happy to be upset. Thank you, Fang-fang."

Of course, the result was wonderful, and every one was happy. Liu got along with Apple very well afterward, so did Fang-fang and I. We soon became very good friends with her.

When Spring Festival, the Chinese New Year, came, we had a splendid reunion dinner on Eve at home and everyone, my parents, Fang-fang and I, went to bed after the clock struck twelve, which meant ringing out the Old and ringing in the New.

The following day, when I told Fang-fang two of my roommates, Andi and Lim, would come over for dinner, she insisted that she would leave to visit Liu in the evening, no matter how hard I tried to persuade her to stay.

"How can I explain to them? They know you are here, and they all want to meet you."

"I'm not an exhibit," she said impatiently. "I hate to be shown off for anyone's purpose."

"Oh, come on! Do you think I only want to show off?" I said. Something in her tone annoyed me. I didn't know what made her act so unreasonably. "It's up to you if you want to leave."

"I'm sorry," she said at last. "I didn't mean to upset you. But I just can't stay cozily with someone I don't know."

"All right, do as you please."

135

"Please understand me."

When I met her eyes, begging to be excused, what could I say? I could only let her go with my understanding, an unwillingly understanding.

Andi and Lim weren't happy. They complained about the boring life at school during the winter vacation: without dance, without girls, without fun, without excitement, without anything but enough time for sleeping.

"I can't even imagine having to stay at school next winter," Lim said. "I should save some money from my mouth and buy me a ticket next time."

"It's unrealistic," Andi said. "You would starve to death if you tried to save money from your mouth."

"I have four younger brothers and sisters. It's very hard for my parents to support me and other four kids. If I can find a part-time job, I prefer to work for my own living expenses."

"Me too," Andi. "I hate to be a burden on my parents when I'm already twenty."

"The government should let us work. We have hands, and we don't want to be a dependent."

"It's a dream anyway," Lim said. "We have to ask our parents for money and we have to depend on them."

"Why don't you enjoy yourselves? Holding a dance, or a weekend party for you remainders?"

"That's not easy, you know. We are scattered everywhere on the campus. It's very hard to be in contact. And, there are only a few girls left, nowhere near enough for dance partners."

"Maybe you can come and visit me more often."

"No, we can't. If we visit you, we have to change three buses on one way, and it takes more than an hour. I never saw such a crowded bus before in my life. You can't even move an arm or leg when you are in it."

"We are not built for getting on the Shanghai bus anyway."

"All right, all right. Then you can only stay on campus."

"Sleeping day and night."

6

Wu didn't have a good time in winter vacation either, maybe
worse than Andi and Lim. Andi asked him anxiously as soon as
Wu entered our room on the registration day.

"Is everything Ok?"

"No," Wu said depressingly.

"What on earth is it? Are you divorced or not?" Andi went
in hot pursuit and didn't even let Wu take a breath.

"No."

"Why?" We all turned our eyes to him.

"She wasn't ready to," he said. When he finally sat down on
his bed, he added, "She said she preferred to die if I wanted to
divorce with her."

"Wow!"

His wife's family, in which two sons were local cadres, was a
powerful clan in the village. They married their daughter to Wu
only because she was a substandard old maid. They looked down
upon Wu's family, which was nothing but poor, even when Wu
became the first college student in their village. When the family
learned that Wu was going to divorce with their daughter, they
burned with huge wrath because they thought it was a shame to
their clan. They gathered a bunch of family members together
and clashed into Wu's house with rods and sticks. They
threatened to destroy the house if Wu didn't take back what he
had said and offer an apology. At this critical moment, Wu's wife
went out of the room and kept her family members off the
house.

"I'll fight to bitter end with you if you dare touch a single
hair of my husband's head," she said with a hoe in her hands.

"But you told us this coward wanted to divorce you," her
father said with rage and a purple face.

"It's none of your business. It's between him and me. I don't
think it's his own will. He's certainly misled by a seductive
woman at his school. When I find out who that whore is, I will
make her pay for it."

"Then give him a warning: if he hurts you, we won't let him
off."

Wu fell in a chair when his in-laws were gone. He knew now
it would be much harder than he expected if he wanted to get
rid of his wife. It would cause bloodshed at least. He looked at
his old parents who were terribly frightened and made up his
mind at last that he couldn't let his parents be hurt again.

"Maybe it will pass peacefully," he said. "But I'm not quite sure. My wife is a narrow-minded woman."

"So you gave up already," Andi said.

"What could I do?" he said. "Maybe I should wait for several years, till she's bored with living alone."

"She will never be bored," Four-eyes said. "All she wants is living creditably under the roof of her husband's house. She won't care if the house is empty. I saw lots of miserable women like her in the countryside. They thought divorce was the most shameful thing in the world. They preferred live separately rather than be divorced."

"I know. But I have to think of my poor parents who are extremely helpless in our village."

"Maybe you can get rid of your wife when your parents pass away someday," Fu said.

"My God! How long he should wait?" Andi said.

"Why don't you go to the court," I said. "It's illegal to disregard personal safety."

"You know nothing when you're only twenty-six and live peacefully so far away in a big city," Four-eyes said. "Her family are local bullies, who can shut out the heavens with one hand if they want to."

"Then go to the county court, to the province . . ." Andi said.

"Don't be childish, Andi," Fu said. "Who cares about such a tiny case as an internal conflict in a family? There are a great many matters more serious than divorce that remain carelessly in the files of county or province court."

"Do you mean Wu can do nothing about it?" Lim asked.

"I'm afraid not," Fu said.

Wu had been sitting on his bed depressed while we were arguing about his business. He knew what Four-eyes and Fu said was true; for his whole life, he had to live with his unloving wife.

Not long after the semester began, the political instructor in our class came to Wu and had a serious talk with him. The political instructor was the secretary of the Party branch, whose function was dealing with the ideological problems in our students. He told Wu that his wife had lodged a complaint against him. She said her husband would be another Chen Shimei if the Party didn't redeem him in time. A thousand years ago there was a man named Chen Shimei who tried to forsake his wife when he became a governor. His name became a synonym for those who tried to break their wedding vows when they were in a higher position. The opinion of the political instructor was very clear. None of his students could be a Chen Shimei because we were the first term of students after the Cultural Revolution, and we couldn't do anything wrong.

138

So Wu was forced to write a self-criticism and had to promise he wouldn't go to court with his wife, at least while he was at school. This event became an incident that touched off a comprehensive campaign against the corrosive influence of bourgeois ideology in the campus. We were told that all the college students were the pride of our Party and people, so we could never bring shame on them. Forsaking a wife certainly was a shame.

Wu got a hard stroke in a word. For almost a whole month, he didn't dare appear at any dance parties because he couldn't let anyone think he was interested in girls or looking for a girl-friend—his wife believed he had one. "If I had been hesitating, I'm not hesitating now," he said one day. "Whenever I have the chance, I will divorce with her. She is too smart to be forgiven."

"They won't let you do that here, you know," Fu said.

"I can wait," he said.

"Poor Wu," Fang-fang said when she knew the story. "Common customs are thick walls which you can never destroy."

"If millions of people push the wall together," I said. "There's nothing they can't conquer."

"Easier said than done."

She still didn't invite me to her dorm room although we often met on campus. And she never went with me in public. Sometimes if we ran into each other on our way, she only said hello to me as if we were normal schoolmates. But as soon as we stayed together in secret, she would tear off her indifference and become extremely hot and sexy. Sometimes I was amazed at her duality, which always confused me. In fact, she was a great actress who acted just right.

In the middle of the semester, when it was time to reelect the deputy of the National People's Congress, there was a movement of democracy arising quietly in the campus. Some of the students advanced a clarion call that we should have real democracy and have our own deputy. In spite of the fact that the deputy had been selected by organizations at all levels for last thirty years, they wanted to select their own deputy now.

Four-eyes was an activist for democracy. He said the first thing that should be reformed in China was the system of election; and China should learn from western countries for using the fairest campaigning system of election.

"I think the system of campaigning for election doesn't fit the condition of China," Fu said. "Maybe we can do it ten years later, but not now. Now we are only on the first step of reform, and we can't jump too fast. Campaigning should be the last step of reform."

"I can't agree with that," Four-eyes said. "Because the electoral law is the basic law. You can't change anything if you don't change your basic law first. Now the deputies are pets of the top leaders who reflect the official's will, not ours. We need our own deputy who can represent our thinking."

"I know you are right," I said. "No free election, no democracy. But how can we handle an election contest when it never happened before in China?"

"Just do it. Some people have to be pioneers."

"I will be your aid if you enter into the contest," Andi said to Four-eyes. "I've read some reports about running for the presidency in America; and I know how to help you win."

"Then tell us first how can you help him?" Wu said. He never trusted Andi because Andi was too young. "Something in the newspaper is totally different from something that happens in reality. Moreover, the condition of United States is totally different from the condition of China. You can't copy indiscriminately the experience of others."

"So what is your opinion, Wu?" Lim asked.

"I think we should seek a way which fits both sides."

"It sounds like a fairy tale," Four-eyes said. "Is there any way in the world can fits both sides? For example, is there any way in the world to accommodate both your wife and you when you want to divorce but she doesn't?"

Wu immediately lowered his head said, "No."

"So, we can only have one choice, keep the old system or change it, which concerns the success or failure of reform."

"It sounds like success or failure hinges on one action," Fu said.

"I mean it," Four-eyes said. "Reform would be idle talk without democracy. Yet the first step of democracy is giving our people the real rights of election."

"I agree with you," Andi said.

"I agree with one of your opinions," Fu said. "Reform would be idle talk without democracy, yet giving people the rights of election isn't the first step of democracy. The first step should be freedom of speech."

"They are not contradictory," Four-eyes said. "Freedom of speech or the right of election, they are all the basic rights of people. No freedom of speech, no rights of election; conversely, the same."

"Don't you think it's getting late now?" Wu yawned loudly in the darkness. "You have enough time to argue tomorrow."

So the argument kept going for a long time. Gradually, Four-eyes seemed to prevail upon all of us, except Fu, who still thought it was a jump. But he agreed that if Four-eyes entered into the contest, all of us should take part on his behalf, because whether or not he won, it would be a good beginning of reform.

Four-eyes started to get busy with establishing ties and advocating his point of view, while we brought people we knew into contact with him. After two years of boring college life, it was the first time we didn't devote the full energy to textbooks or tests but share some with other business.

When summer vacation came, the movement of democracy had swept across the campus. Most of students were aroused as well as professors.

"In fall," Four-eyes said before he left for vacation. "You will see the most exciting scene on our campus."

7

The fire of reform was spreading widely. When I called on my friends before school was over, I found Ge and Bamboo Pole were working as contractors, while Big Liu had become a student in the evening college, in which each student could be a worker, clerk, or anything else during the day time. When student graduated from evening college three years later, he could get a college diploma and could be engaged by the company.

"I'm sorry, Li Ling," Ge said. "I can't leave right now. We just started, and I'm trying to find out which way is the best for us to go. Bamboo is the same. Maybe Big Liu could travel with you."

"No," Big Liu said. "I can't. The time is too pressing since I have been taking the work-study program at the evening college. I have to work as well as take courses. It's really hard for me."

"All right," I said. "It seems I'm the only one who could enjoy the summer now."

"I wish I could go with you," Bamboo Pole said. "But I just made contract with the company two months ago, and everything isn't in the right path yet."

"I know. Maybe we can go together next summer."

"Yes," Ge said. "Next summer, everything will be on the right track and I will go with you."

"Me too," Bamboo Pole said.

"Ok, keep your words."

I visited Ge and Bamboo Pole's shops afterward. The exterior of the shops hadn't changed any, but the interior was different. In addition to selling rice and flour and noodles, they now opened up many new supplies of goods: corns, millet, red bean, boy-bean, peanuts, etc.

"How could you get these supplies?" I asked.

"Oh, it's a hard job," Ge said. "I went everywhere I could to find the source, then beg, request, and ask for help. I'll tell you something, Li Ling. How much I have here, and how much sweat I spent."

"It needs both time and money," Bamboo Pole said. "You have to go through private channels and give dinners or send gifts. Now you can't get anything through the normal channels."

"Can you still make more profit?"

"Sure. The first month we made double, this month we made three times more than before," Ge said.

"Almost," Bamboo Pole said.

"Then how much do you earn?"

"Ha," Ge said triumphantly. "Much more than your college graduates. About two hundred."

"Oh!" College graduates could only get sixty the first year, seventy to eighty the second year. Two hundred was a professor's salary.

"Including bonus," Bamboo Pole added.

"So I'd better go back to the rice shop when I graduate and work as a contractor." As I said, I felt somewhat distressed. Before the Cultural Revolution, the financial status of the working class and the intellectual were almost even, although the working class had better political treatment. In the Revolution, the political position of the two classes was divided into two opposing extremes. Now, the financial status was changing. A worker's salary was equal to a professor's; and a trader's one month's profit was equal to the intellectual specialist's whole year's income. I didn't know what would happen if this trend continued. At very least our children wouldn't want to be intellectuals.

Before I went to my friends, I had invited Fang-fang to travel with us. Now they left the two of us to make our plans. I wanted to go Yellow Mountain again, but she wanted to climb up the Taishan Mountain. Before we made up our minds, Liu came with Apple and asked if they could go with us. We were happy to have them, and we all agreed to climb up Taishan Mountain, the symbol of emperors in ancient times.

Taishan had been a place where the emperors paid homage to the Heaven and the Earth. Many historic sites remained on the way from the foot to the top. Since it was a holy mountain in ancient China, the rocky stairs were neat and wide, and the installations were perfect and diversified. Having climbed up the Yellow Mountain, clambering up Taishan Mountain seemed like walking on the street to me. Moreover, Fang-fang had been introducing and explaining every historic site on our way while we were walking. It really was fun. She knew almost every detail of these ancient temples, buildings, archways and trees. "I just wonder how can you know so much," I said.

"I've read the guide-book," she said.

"I've read it too," Liu said. "It didn't tell me anything."

"Don't forget my major is Chinese," she smiled.

"Oh, yes! You should know more than we do," I said.

We stopped at Zhongtianmen, the door on the half way to the Heaven and had lunch at a small inn.

"What luxury," I said. "We could even have a beer."

"It's the first time I've been so far away from home," Apple said.

"It will be your best experience, you know," Liu said. "Traveling with two handsome young men and a beautiful female

143

scholar. Who else in the world has such luck?"

"I would be luckier if you were not as chatty as a sparrow," she responded.

Upward from Zhongtianmen was the most scenic part of the mountain. Huge pine trees and cypresses were reaching to the sky while milky white clouds lazily moved around the peaks. Ravines were roaring with swift streams. Everything in Taishan Mountain was grand and heavy, even the stones, solid, tough and sturdy. The shadow of the trees was so wide and thick, it almost covered everything.

But the enjoyment of the natural beauty paled when we stepped towards Nantianmen, the south door of the Heaven. There were hundreds and thousands of steps leading up to a huge decorated archway on which three golden Chinese characters shone in the sun. It was the top of Taishan Mountain, yet the endless flight of the steps frightened us all. The archway seemed too far to reach.

We climbed mechanically. Liu and I carried all the packs. Instead of joking and laughing, there were panting and sweating.

"Oh, my God!" Every time when we stopped and took a short break, Apple would look up at the archway and ask, "How many more steps shall we climb? One thousand more or two thousand more?"

"I really don't know," Liu would answer. "We need another half an hour I think."

"Oh, my God!" she cried. "Another!"

"Are you Ok?" I asked Fang-fang.

"I'm all right," she said. "Give me the bag, Li Ling, it's too heavy for you."

"It's all right."

Nantianmen was unattainably high to us. We were busy walking, panting, sighing, complaining, anything but enjoying the great scenes under our feet. When we finally arrived the top of the mountain after two hours working on these endless steps, we were all awed by its magnificent and majestic appearance, with a view that seemed to extend hundreds and thousands of miles, steady and shady, full of power and grandeur.

"Oh, my God! I'm exhausted," Apple sighed and leaned on Liu for support.

"Hold out," Liu said. "We should look for a hotel first."

"Go ahead," I said. "I prefer to stay here for a while."

Fang-fang and I were standing behind the archway, looking down the mountain. Far below, the tourists were crawling like ants on the steps. The cool wind sent a shiver running over my body. I took Fang-fang's hand and said, "You see, people downstairs are as tiny as ants, and so are we if they look up at us. A poet said when you are on top of the mountain you feel like a drop in the ocean. The world is so big!"

"It is unpredictable too. Just like the clouds in the sky, we never know where we will go."

I looked at her. Her face was sad.

"Li Ling! Fang-fang! Come here!" Liu shouted at us somewhere.

"We are coming," I yelled back. "Do you find any place?" I asked when I saw them standing in front of a temple.

"Here is a hotel," Liu said. "But we can't live here."

"It's too dirty inside," his girl said. "All the quilts are wet, so wet that you can wring out water from them."

"But it is the only hotel on the top, you know," Fang-fang said.

"Yes, I know. But how can we sleep with wet quilts all night long?"

"What do you think, Li Ling?" Liu asked.

"Maybe we can look for some private inns at the back of the mountain," I said. "We used to live with villagers in Yellow Mountain. It's a wonderful experience."

"All right, let's go."

It's very easy to find a place to spend the night in Taishan Mountain. Almost every big house you passed could provide you a room if you asked. We soon found a house beside a creek. The hosts were a middle-aged couple who rented us two rooms, and each of the rooms cost only five yuan a night.

I had hesitated for awhile when I allotted the rooms. Frankly, I preferred to stay with Fang-fang rather than with Liu. But I couldn't. Not because I was afraid to tell Liu that we had had sex already, but because Apple was so young and so pure, and I didn't know if she could accept the arrangement to sleep with Liu.

So I finally stayed with Liu while Apple stayed with Fang-fang. I heard them talking and laughing inside the room, but I was so tired that I soon fell into a deep sleep.

The next day we discussed where we would go after a breakfast of some soybean milk and steaming breads at a pastry stall not far from the house.

"Maybe we can be separated for half a day," Fang-fang said. "You can go south while Li Ling and I will go west. We'll meet at lunch time and exchange information if we see something remarkable on our way."

"That's a wonderful idea," Liu responded at once. "If we find something interesting, we will let you know."

I knew he wanted to stay with his girl alone, but I didn't know why Fang-fang acted so impetuously. We had been together before we left for this trip.

As soon as we walked into a tract of thick trees, she immediately turned to me and said, "Oh, Li Ling, I just can't stand it."

145

"Stand what?"

"When you are at my side but I can't touch you."

"Poor darling," I kissed her and said. "I miss you too."

"I couldn't even sleep last night."

"It's only a few days, you know. When we leave for your home two days from now, we will have plenty of time to stay together."

"Oh, no." She got herself free from my hug and said. "You can't go with me, Li Ling. My mother is an old-fashioned woman who would be mad if she knew something."

"But we can cover up, can't we?"

"You know we can't," she became very nervous. "I can never keep my feelings secretly if you are with me."

"All right, all right. I won't go this time. But you should at least let me visit your mother once before we get married."

"We can never get married, Li Ling. I told you thousand times already. We have to be separated as soon as we graduate."

"What a nonsense! Do you think I will give up? No. You are mine. I will go with you wherever you go and marry you." I became excited and my fanatic kissing made her lean against me in my arms. She cried a little when I unbuttoned her and weighed her down on the stony ground.

"It would be so nice if we can always stay together like this," she murmured when she lay beside me.

"We will," I said and kissed her softly.

"Anyway, it would be the sweetest memory in my mind." She stroked my chest with her tender fingers and her voice became an echo far away from me. "Will you remember me, Li Ling, always?"

I woke up at noon. Fang-fang was sitting beside me when I lifted my heavy eyelids. "It's time for lunch now," she smiled at me. "We should go back to the house."

"How long have I been sleeping?"

"I don't know. Maybe two hours."

"What should we say if they ask us about the scene?"

"You could say nothing special."

I said so when Liu asked me.

"Nothing special on our way too," Apple said. "But we met a local farmer and he said the east side of the mountain is great. Shall we go together after lunch?"

"Sure."

Two days later, we left Taishan. Fang-fang said goodbye to each of us and took an evening train home. We three made a detour to Qūfu where was the birthplace of Confucius. We visited the Confucian Temple, Park, and Manor. Without Fang-fang, the scene seemed dim and dull. So I urged Liu to buy the tickets the next day and went back directly to Shanghai.

I had been longing to go back school since I had come back from Taishan Mountain. Not only because I missed Fang-fang, but because I was interested in the process of the election.

On September 1, the fixed registration day for all schools in Shanghai, I went to our school early in the morning, waiting for my roommates. When Four-eyes finally showed up, all of us immediately gathered around him, asking about the political situation in Peking.

"We can run for an election contest now," he told us. "At Peking University, they already start to work for the final campaign. One of my high school classmate becomes the student campaigner at his school. I went to several debates last week. They were absolutely exciting and heartening."

"When can we start?" Andi asked. He was always so impatient.

"Now," Four-eyes said. "Today."

"How?"

"We can start with doing propaganda. When most of the students on campus are ready, we can stand up for the campaign."

We discussed the details of campaign enthusiastically. When we broke off the discussion for supper in the evening, Four-eyes seemed to remember something and asked Wu, "How about you, Wu? Are you in trouble? You seem very quiet today."

"It's hard to explain," Wu said. "I haven't been home this summer."

"What?"

"I couldn't see her," he said. "I just couldn't stand her."

"Where have you been in the whole summer?"

"Jinan," he said. Jinan was the capital city of Shandong Province. "I've been working for a magazine for two months."

"Did your wife know?"

"Yes."

"What did she say?"

"I don't know. I only called my parents twice and they didn't tell me anything about her."

"You should divorce, anyway," Fu said. But nobody responded. We all knew it wasn't easy, especially in his hometown.

Four-eyes became the first one on our campus who declared that he would run for deputy. To help him win, we put up wall newspapers and organized debates. Our room became the center of movement and Four-eyes was a leader.

The political instructor had tried several times to persuade us to give up at the very beginning, but adopting a laissez-faire attitude afterward when he found out it was already a trend of the time. At the same time, more and more students stood up and responded to us. Every day there were discussions, debates, and other activities around the campus. It was the first time that we didn't go to the dance on Friday but went to the classroom instead.

I never went to dance again since I had sunk into the whirlwind of the election involuntarily. I was too busy. It seemed like I hadn't been to the dance hall for a couple months when Fang-fang finally called on me. She had never called on me before.

"What happened?" I asked. She was very nervous.

"Nothing. I was just worried about you, since you haven't showed up for several weeks."

"Oh!" When I finally knew that she had been waiting for me every Friday night, I felt sorry. "It's my fault," I said. "I should have let you know. But I was too busy to remember anything."

"But you could have told me earlier, couldn't you?"

"Yes, it's my fault, I already told you. But if you had told me your room number, maybe I could have already informed you seven times. But you never let me know your number; I don't know why."

To my surprise, she burst into tears when she heard what I said. "I knew you would act like that someday," she sobbed. "You don't need to be afraid to tell me if you're already tired of me."

"What?" I was shocked. "That's the stupidest thing I ever heard! Get tired of you? Me? Oh, no! I would never get tired of you. You know that, don't you? I love you. You are the only one in the world I want to marry. How could I get tired of you? Listen to me, my dearest. If you are hurt because I didn't show up, I apologize. If you think I didn't show up because I got tired of you, you are wrong."

"I'm sorry, Li Ling. I shouldn't say that. I did it only because I love you too much. Love, this is what I need to hear from you. I love you." She kissed me, and I kissed her. I could never control myself if I hadn't worried about my roommates who might come in at any moment. I promised her that I would do my best to find the time to meet her and dance with her.

But I didn't keep my promise. I didn't show up in following two weeks. The debate became white-hot, and each of us had been spending every minute of our leisure time on it. Every evening, the classrooms in each department building would be bright with lights till lights-out.

Our school was an independent electoral ward in Shanghai, which could have six to ten basic deputies. From these basic deputies, one out of ten could be the city deputy who would go to Peking to elect the top leaders of our country. Since eighty percent of the deputies should be the faculty, only twenty percent could be students. Which meant we, fifteen thousand students altogether, could have no more than two deputies.

The first debate included more than twenty candidates from different departments. After a whole month of fierce rivalry, there were only half of them left.

As Four-eyes' classmates and roommates, we supported him and hoped he would be the winner. During rivalry, even Fu, who still didn't agree with Four-eyes' opinion, was busy with odd jobs of debates.

When the polling day came, we went to the polling booth early in the afternoon and voted for Four-eyes as well as for our civil rights. We anxiously awaited till the result was announced: Four-eyes was the winner!

"Congratulations!" We cheered while Four-eyes shook hands with everyone.

"Oh, great," Andi said loudly and happily. "I can go back to my girl now. In two months, I haven't seen her once!"

My heart sank when I heard what he said. My Lord! I totally forgot Fang-fang! I rushed out of the room, leaving all of them behind.

When I finally met her after three hours waiting, she acted like nothing happened; not even mentioned a word about my failure of keeping my promise. Every time when I tried to explain and apologize, she stopped me by changing the topic.

I knew she was hurt. Her indifferent silence was worse than anger. I knew her. Only when she was deeply hurt, she would act like that. I looked into her eyes but couldn't see anything.

"Please," I caught hold of her arms and stopped her. "Can't you forgive me?"

"It's my fault," she said calmly. "I have no right to ask you to do anything you don't want to."

"I want to be with you, you know that. Now, the election is over and we can be together whenever you want."

"Do you think it's necessary?"

"What do you mean necessary?"

"Shall we meet again when I'm only an obstacle to you?"

"Don't be silly, Fang-fang. I love you. Isn't it perfectly clear?"

She didn't respond me but tears ran down quietly on her face. I held her in my arms and hugged her tightly. "I'm sorry, I didn't mean to hurt you."

"It's my fault," she sobbed. "I love you so much that I'm always afraid I would lose you."

"How could?" I kissed her softly.

"I don't know. I always have a nightmare twining around me. I'm scared."

"Don't worry, darling. If you want, we can marry now."

"No. It's just a foolish thinking. I'll be all right. Don't worry about me."

"Then tell me, darling, can we see each other again twice a week?"

"Yes."

9

Winter vacation was very exciting, because my grandparents came to visit us. Fang-fang went back home this year, as did Andi and Lim. I wasn't sure if Wu would be back or if he still couldn't stand his wife.

My grandparents arrived Shanghai two days before the Chinese New Year. They were going to spend the Spring Festival with us. Time had indelibly marked on their faces. They were old, unchangeably old.

"So glad to see you again, my dear baby," grandma gave me a big hug.

"Call him Li Ling, Mamma," my mother said. "He's a twenty-six year old grown-up now."

"No matter how old he is, he's always my dear little boy." Her eyes were still bright and kind. I couldn't help but say, "Yes, grandma."

She tapped on my hand as if I were a child. "We will have lots of fun," she said. "Your grandpa and I have been looking forward to seeing you for a long time."

My grandpa was smiling when my grandma talked to me. He wore a formal suit and a matching tie. "You're really a big man now," he said and patted my shoulder. "Taller than all of us."

"Yes," my mother laughed. "He's the tallest."

They stayed in Shanghai only a couple of weeks. They complained about the weather, colder than what they could be used to; about the soldiers and the police. I couldn't help laughing when they told me about that.

"They won't hurt you," I said.

"No," my grandpa said seriously. "But I just can't sleep well if there are soldiers in my sight."

Before they left for home, they called me and spoke to me seriously.

"I had discussed with your grandpa before we came here," my grandma said. "We are old, but we still can do something for you. We have a good amount of money in the bank, more than enough to send you to abroad for advanced study. If you want, you can have the money at any time."

"Thank you," I said. "But I don't want to leave now."

"Think of it," grandpa said. "This is a chance which could probably change your life. You could have a splendid future, and you could find a suitable place anywhere in the world for your own. Think of it, Li Ling."

151

"We won't push you," grandma said. "But let us know when you make the decision. We are always there when you need help."

"Oh, I will." I threw myself into her arms. She stroked my hair softly just as she often did when I was a little boy. "Write to us," she said.

"I will."

The following week I kept thinking about the captivating prospect they offered me. I knew going abroad would be the best chance for me and for my future. In our country, one who got a degree abroad could get everything he wanted easier than others—house, position, opportunities and money. A lecturer at our school for example, needed at least ten years to be an associate professor, but a holder of a Ph.D from abroad needed only two years. And going abroad would be an adventure. It would open my eyes, and at least would let me know how other people lived in the world. It was a chance everyone wanted to have.

Yet I couldn't accept it. I had Fang-fang here. She now kept on saying that our marriage was unrealistic because we had to be separated when we graduate. If she knew I would be gone when we graduate, what would she say? I had no choice but to stay. I knew the chance of going abroad was an external thing, while a wife would share in my whole life.

But when I told Fang-fang my decision, she took it personally and seriously. "You shouldn't abandon such a good chance for me," she said.

"That's all right. I've made the decision. If I go abroad, I will go with you."

"Don't be childish, Li Ling. The opportunity won't always be there. If our country' policy changed someday, or if the door closed again, you would lose it forever."

"I won't regret it," I said, "if I can live with you forever. I love you, Fang-fang. I can marry nobody but you."

"We can never be married," she said, "if you throw away your future because of me."

"Why?"

"Because I would never forgive myself."

"Then we'll go together."

"No. It's impossible. My major is Chinese. Do you want me to learn Chinese from some other country?"

"You can change your major," I said.

"What else can I learn? You know I would never change my major."

"So I won't go anyway. We will be married, and you will be my wife. The distance can't be an obstacle. Wherever you go after school, I will go with you."

Her eyes stared at me worriedly. "Why must you be as

stubborn as a stone? If I die someday, what would you do?"

"Maybe I would go abroad then," I said jokingly.

She smiled bitterly and sighed.

"Don't be depressed, my dear." I drew her into my arms. "You should be happy because you have such a loyal and devoted boy-friend."

"But I'm not sure if I can be happy." She cuddled lie into my arms.

I became excited when I touched her soft and warm body. We were too impatient to wait to kiss each other. She clung to me tightly while my hand moved slowly under her thick clothes on her curves. Huge flakes of flame came over me, burning my mind. The hand over her became nervous and rubbed her breasts harder and harder. She moaned and her hands unbuttoned my pants. She lay down on the ground and my body covered hers. At that moment, the only thought in my mind was having her. But I knew I shouldn't. The early spring in our town was cold and I couldn't let her lie naked on the ice-cold ground. And, I didn't have a condom with me.

But the fire of lust was burning, and I became a robot. I couldn't control myself anymore. I was yearning for her, but I had to struggle to calm myself down. My excitement was getting the way. I couldn't do it well. My penis was painful, and I struggled very hard.

Suddenly, I felt a hand holding my penis and rubbing it. I cried, not because it hurt me but because it made me happy beyond description. "Oh, yes!" I cried. "Please don't stop! Oh, yes . . ."

I didn't know how long she had been working. I had been lying down on the ground while she was kneeling beside. I felt her hand on and off, on and off, might be stopped at any moment. I became nervous. I couldn't help it. I wanted to be finished before she stopped, but I couldn't. I tried very hard, but I couldn't. I cried and trembled, but couldn't do me any good. Then I felt something touch my lips, a little bit itchy, but very comfortable. I opened my eyes and saw her bare breasts touching my face. I bit her nipples and sucked hard. She burst out crying and her hand on my penis moved quickly. As soon as we finished, we were sweating all over our bodies.

"Oh, my God," she was panting. "You exhausted me."

I laughed and started to kiss her.

She closed her eyes and murmured, "If we could have a child someday, it would be perfect."

"We will," I said while kept kissing. "If you like, we can have ten kids."

She laughed then suddenly serious, she opened her eyes and stared at me. "I would like to have your child."

"You should have it!" I said jokingly and teased her with my kissing and stroking. "I can give it to you right now if you want."

"Oh, no," she moaned. "You are teasing me. It's not fair . . . Oh, please, please . . ." she cried and wrenched her body, while her hand held my soft penis and rubbed it.

"Oh, that's enough, my dear," I felt something in my body change and I knew I would lose my mind if she kept doing it. "It's dangerous!" She knew that I didn't bring any safety tool with me and she knew how painful it would be for me if I couldn't have her when I was aroused.

But she was still working.

I was aroused beyond bearing it. There was no longer any choice for me. I went over her and made it. In the whole process, she had been exciting my deepest lust.

"Fang-fang, my dear," I called her carefully. She was lying on the ground as if she had fallen asleep. "Are you all right?"

"Yes," she said quietly. Under the dim light of the new moon, I saw tears silently running down her pale face.

"Fang-fang!" I shook her. "Are you all right?"

"Yes," she opened her eyes and answered me. "I'm all right."

"But you're crying."

"Am I?" she forced a smile. "Maybe I'm too exhausted."

"I was afraid I hurt you," I held her into my arms. "I'm sorry. I shouldn't be so impatient."

"I like that," she said and kissed me. "I love you and always will."

"I love you too." I stroked her beautiful hair and said. "You can take some pills if it's dangerous."

"Don't worry," she said calmly. "It's safe."

"Are you sure?"

"Yes."

The door was closed when we came back school.

"Oh, it's almost two o'clock in the morning!" she said when she looked at her watch under the streetlights.

"Well, we have to climb over the wall now, my crazy girl," I said.

"Oh, yes. We have to. I don't want to let my roommates think I'm missing."

"Maybe they would think you are sleeping with me," I said.

"Yes." She said and drew me quickly away from the door.

10

Nobody knew that we had climbed over the wall at midnight; not even the gate-watcher of our school. Later, we often made a date away from school in the evenings, but never again as late as that night.

Three weeks later, Fang-fang went back to Anhui once because her mother was ill. She stayed with her mother for a couple of days then came back school again.

While she was out of the school, the wall of democracy, where people discussed the politics of our country and expressed their own opinions was demolished in Peking.

"The government wanted to eliminate the wall for a long time," Four-eyes said.

"The wall wasn't harmful anyway," Andi said. "I just don't understand why they couldn't leave it alone."

"They said the wall has confused people and poisoned people's mind."

"Governments always want to have their own way," Fu said. "Not a single exception in the world."

"They should know that when one person has the say, it's the hotbed of the *autocracy*," Four-eyes said.

"I'm afraid you will be in trouble soon," Wu said. "The crushed wall is a signal."

"Why?" Lim asked.

"If they don't like democracy, they won't like campaigning."

"I know," Four-eyes said. "They won't allow us to have personal rights of democracy and freedom."

"Maybe it won't be as serious as you thought," I said.

"Maybe," he said. "But I won't cherish illusions."

His worry came true. Not long after, he became a target of the movement ferreting out the men who used to run around on sinister errands during the Cultural Revolution; then he was criticized for his political views in the campaign, which suggested a possibility of treason against the leadership of the Communist Party. Because he used to be a Red Guard when he was in high school, he was subjected to the censure of opinion of our school and they found fault with him campaigning, accusing him of having an axe to grind.

The one good thing that came of this was that he didn't need to go to any political study classes. The political study classes and public accusation meetings were swept together with the Cultural Revolution into the garbage can.

He was only criticized by name in some cadres' speech. At the same time, our political instructor had been talking with him for couple weeks, trying to persuade him to give up his political views and make a self-criticism. Four-eyes certainly wouldn't give up. They confronted each other for a month, then ended up with nothing definite. But we all knew Four-eyes was in trouble now. They wouldn't let him off. The Party cadres would make reprisals; they always did. At least, Four-eyes wouldn't get a good job when he graduated.

"I don't care," he said when we asked him what was he going to do if they make reprisals against him. "I don't need them to offer me a job."

"So what will you do? You can't live without a job, can you?"

"No. But I can get a job myself. I'm going to leave. I will seek my democracy and freedom outside of China."

"So you dare to do whatever you want," Wu said. "If I had leeway as you do, I wouldn't care anything."

"I know leaving isn't a glorious way for me," Four-eyes said. "I wouldn't take it if I had another choice. But the situation didn't allow me to have any opportunity."

The room was full of unbearable silence. We knew he was right; he had no choice but leaving. But the way he had to chose seemed like sneaking away.

"Everyone can make his own choice," Fu said at last. "Four-eyes at least has done something."

"Yes, I know," Wu said.

During the time when Four-eyes was being criticized, I met Fang-fang as usual, but all our meetings were overshadowed by the event. Every time when we were together, I couldn't help but mention Four-eyes again and again. Fang-fang was interested in what I told her too. She listened quietly, and asked me questions.

I didn't notice that she was getting thinner and thinner till one day when she suddenly threw up when we were talking. "What's the matter?" I held her shoulders and found out they were emaciated. "Are you sick?"

"No . . . yes. I've got stomach trouble," she said weakly.

"I'll send you to the doctor," I said. In the campus, there was a health center in which all our students could get public health services.

"No. It will be all right. Don't worry."

"How long have you been sick? You look so pale."

"About a week. I got a flu, I think."

"A week? Why didn't you tell me?"

"Oh, nothing serious, Li Ling."

"Let's go back to school. You need to lie down and relax."

She let me send her back to the dorm building. "I'm all right now," she said. "Don't worry about me."

"Be a good girl," I said. "I'll see you tomorrow."

"I'll be all right. See you next week."

"Are you sure?"

"Yes."

"All right. See you next week."

The next week she told me she had recovered. Although her face was still pale, she stopped getting thinner. Moreover, the passion of love seemed to go back her again. So I believed she was all right.

Spring was coming to the end. Now it was Chinese Labor Day. We could have a long weekend in the beginning of May. So we finally took a midnight train and arrived Shuzhou, the nearest town in the morning.

May was the best time to travel. The sky was bright blue, the fields were green, and the flowers were everywhere. The numerous narrow rivers and tiny lakes that intricately laced the Shuzhou area were olive green. Even the villages were greenyellow with trees and household plants. In this green world, the air was fresh and the smell was nice. We carried a small bag, strolling along in the lovely town.

Shuzhou was one of the oldest cities in China, famous for its ancient gardens and parks built in Ming and Qing Dynasties.

Of all the gardens we had seen, I like West Park (Xiyuan) best, where a tiny garden connected with a huge temple.

The Hall of Arhat was the most distinguished place in West Park. There were five hundred arhats sitting or standing, various in shapes, lifelike and vivid. A characteristic one in those five hundred arhats was Jigong, a lunatic monk who always helped the distressed and poor people, dressed in rags and barefoot, with a torn cattail leaf fan in the right hand. Whenever you looked at his face, you would admire the great skill of ancient artists. The expression of Jigong was magnificent. You could never say what his face exactly looked like because what you saw depended on where you were. If you looked at him on the right side, it was a laughing Jigong, but if you looked at him from left side, it would be a suffering Jigong. If you looked at him in front, it was a lunatic monk with a faint smile.

Fang-fang was surprised when she caught sight of him. She kept changing her position, as curious as a child. "What an inconceivable creation!" she cried. "I can't imagine how could they make his face like that. Intelligence!"

"Do you want to know your luck?" I asked.

"Yes. How?"

"Men left, women right. If you want to know your luck of this year, you should turn right as soon as you enter the hall and count from the beginning. You are twenty-seven, so the twenty-seventh arhat on the right side would be your omen of your luck."

"What about you?"

"I should turn left when I enter the hall."

"How can I read my luck if I find my arhat?"

"Read the expression on his face. If he's smiling, you will have good luck; if he's pulling a long face, you might be in trouble soon."

"Oh, really?"

She immediately turned right and looked for her omen arhat on the right side.

"Tell me, Li Ling. What does that mean?"

She pointed an arhat who leaned against a wall and his face was blank as pool of dead water.

"I can't read it," I said. "Maybe you need lots sleep; or maybe you should think a lot."

"Is that right?"

"Believe it or not, depending on your own judgment."

"Let's go see your omen arhat," she said.

We went back to the door, then counted from left. "Here he is," I said. We stopped in front of an arhat who sat cross-legged and whose eyebrows knitted. It had a painful looking face with a worried frown.

"Very bad luck," I said jokingly. "I will be suffering soon."

"No, no!" She cried, and her face as white as a paper. "It's not true." She looked at me, and her eyes were blank with despair. "Tell me, it's not true."

"No, it's not true. I'm just joking." I was surprised, and I couldn't understand why she was overreacting so.

"Don't worry about me, my dear," I said to her. "It's only a legend. I've never had any faith in it. Anyway, how could I be suffering? I'm the luckiest man in the world. Come on, give me a smile."

11

We had to leave Shuzhou at night because no hotel would take us as a couple. We found a small town in the suburbs. A narrow street was the guts of it, asphalt crumbling into gravel. Dust rose like breath every time a car or truck passed. We stopped in front of a private inn, which stood at the back side of the street.

"Can I help you?" A fat woman about forty sitting behind a desk, asked listlessly.

"We want a room," I said.

"Do you have marriage certificates?"

"No."

Her eyes shone as if a cat found a mouse. "Twenty per night. Pay first," she said after her eyes had measured both of us up and down.

"All right," I said. I had already read the price on the wall as soon as we entered. It said the highest price was eight yuan per night. But I could do nothing about it because we weren't married, and we wanted to stay together. The owner certainly knew it too.

I gave her two 10-yuan bills, and she gave me a key. "Second door on your left," she said.

The room was simple and crude. A wooden king-sized bed, a table, two chairs, that's all. I turned on the only light in the room and drew up the curtains. Under the dim light of the room, Fang-fang seemed exhausted.

"Sit here," I let her sit down on the bed. "I'll ask the fat woman to bring you some hot water." In these private inns, there was no bathroom.

I brought her one bottle of hot water and a washbasin. "Wash your feet with hot water," I said. "You'll feel better."

"Thank you," she said and took off her shoes and washed. She was very slow in her movements, especially when she bent over to wash her feet.

"Are you all right?"

"Yes."

I waited for her to finish. Then she stood up and looked at me. Her eyes were shining with a strange expression. "Shall we?" I motioned toward the bed. She nodded silently.

I helped her take off her clothes, a jacket, a shirt, and a brassiére. I had been holding my breath as I unbuttoned her little by little, but I still couldn't help but be shocked when her swollen breasts jumped out of their fetters like two balls. They were absolutely new looking; full and solid. I was burning with fierce passion instantly when my hands touched them. I was so eager to feel them that I couldn't wait to put her down on the bed.

Her reaction was strange. As soon as my hands started to rub her breasts, she cried out as if she was hurt. "Oh, no! . . . Oh, please, please don't rub me too hard," she cried painfully.

"Why? Don't you like it, my dear?"

Her struggle stirred my lust more and more and I was very quickly coming to climax. I worked, in and out, and I moaned excitedly.

"Oh, no!" she screamed when I went deeply in her, and her hands tried to resist my advances. Yet, everything she did could only make me more excited. She gave up at last, lying under my body limply.

I saw two lines of tears running down her face. I stopped. "Why?" I kissed her softly. "Did I hurt you?"

She said nothing but used her hands to cover her breasts. "Why? You never felt hurt before. You told me you like to be touched."

"But not now," she said.

"Why?"

She closed her eyes for a while, then drew a deep breath and said, "I'm pregnant."

"Really?"

She nodded and stared at me.

"How long?"

"Three months."

"Oh!" I sat beside her and my eyes measured her bare body inch by inch. I really couldn't accept the fact that she was pregnant. She always took pills when we made love. It's impossible for her to be pregnant. But she was. I knew it when I looked at her body. She had become awkwardly fat, and her breasts were no longer soft and pear-like. She had been changed, changed into a woman, a fat, pregnant woman.

"No!"

"Yes, I am. You know I am."

"Is it mine?" I asked carefully, although I knew the answer would be in the affirmative.

"No."

"What?"

"It's not yours," she said clearly.

"Why? Are you kidding?"

"No."

First, I couldn't accept the fact that she was pregnant, and now I was absolutely stunned and acted like an idiot who was senseless and slow-witted.

"Whose?"

"My husband's."

"Your husband?"

"Yes."

"Are you married."

"Yes."

"Who is the man?"

"Remember the story I told you. The day when I was dying, a neighbor came and helped my mother to move me into his house. Since then, we had been living together. Three years later, I married his son, a young man three years older than I. He is my husband."

"Why didn't you tell me before?"

"I tried to, I told you we could never be married, but you just refused to take my hint."

"How could I? I think I am the only one you love."

"Yes. You are the only one I love."

"Then why don't you divorce your husband?"

"I can't."

"Why?"

"I can't hurt him."

"But you can hurt me, eh?" I burst like an ignited firecracker. "You don't care if you lie to me, lure me, tease me. I'm only your substitute, because you can't live without a man!"

She huddled with fright. "No, Li Ling. It's not true. I love you!" she cried like a child.

"Then divorce him," I held her into my arms. Her tears melt my hatred. I knew she loved me, and I couldn't live without her. "If you want to have this baby, you can have it. I'll treat it as my own child. I'll love both of you."

"Oh, I can't. How can I hurt the man who has save my life? How can I hurt the family that helped us when we were suffering? I owe them, and I owe my husband too much. It's my fate, and nobody can change it. Oh, forgive me, Li Ling; and forget me!"

"No. You can't leave me!"

"You know I have to. I'm married and we have children."

"Children?"

"Yes. We already have a daughter. This will be the second one."

I loosened my grip unconsciously and stared at her as if I had never known her before. "Tell me why?" I murmured.

She was crying. Her tearful eyes looked at me sadly. "I don't want to lose you, I love you."

"But you prefer to live with your unloved husband."

"I just can't, I owe him."

"Are you going to ruin your whole life only because you owed him once? You need love, not to pay a debt. You can't play with your own feelings."

Her tears fell like heavy rain. I put my hand on her shoulder and kissed her wet face. "Listen to me, Fang-fang. I'll go with you to Anhui and tell your husband the truth. If he loves you, he certainly won't stand in the way of your having a happier life."

"No," she shook her head and cried.

"No! No! No! Why don't you think of *me* for once?"

"I can only beg you to forgive me. I know I hurt you, but I didn't do it intentionally. You are the only one I have loved in my whole life. I wish you success and a splendid future. I know you will."

"I don't want to have a splendid future," I said. "I only want you."

"No. I can't have you; and you can't have me. We belong to two different worlds. Forget me, and go abroad. I'll pray for you every day for your success."

"No. If you're leaving me only because of this, I tell you again, I won't go abroad without your companionship."

"Don't be childish, Li Ling. You know the status of our country. It's impossible for me to be divorced. You can read the result from Wu. You know he's hopeless, so do I. I don't want you to be involved in this meaningless dispute that will consume your whole life. Don't worry about me," she held up her forefinger to lock my lips. "I have this child now, and I will live happily in rest of my life."

I looked at her suspiciously. "Do you mean you have *our* child?"

"No. It is mine. I conceived it after I went back home last time," she said calmly.

"Is the time your mother was sick?"

"Yes."

"But you'd just slept with me before you went to his bed," I said as if swallowing a dead fly.

"Yes," she lowered her head and said. "What could I do, though?"

"I just can't understand you," I said. The feeling of being hurt came back to me again. "How could you sleep with a man you don't love? I could never make love with a girl I don't love."

"Do you think I enjoy it?" Her face was twisted. "He is my husband. If I refused him, he certainly would know something. I don't want you to be involved in any trouble on my account." She cried again, and her tears made me nervous.

"What do you want to do now? They won't let you live in the campus once when you are showing."

"I know. I'm going back home at the end of the semester."

"Then go back again afterward?"

"No. I'll transfer to Anhui University afterward. I can live with my mother and take care of my child myself."

162

"So you already made the decision."

"Yes. It will be the last time we are together. I don't know if we can ever see each other again."

She looked at me sadly and her look made me feel bad. Every time my eyes touched her sad wet face, the hatred in my heart melted. I couldn't hate her, I just couldn't. I was like a puppet who could never keep the strings in his own hand.

I held her in my arms silently. She hugged me, and her hot body touched mine. When I woke up the following day, we were still holding each other tightly.

I saw her get up and put on her clothes one by one. The impulse of sex had left me forever.

"Oh, Li Ling," she cried and threw herself on me. "If you want, you still can have me." She took my hand and put it on her breasts. I could feel her trembling when my fingers touched her nipple. I closed my eyes and sighed, "Don't blame yourself too hard, my dear, it's not only your fault."

She cried and let herself go at last.

"You hate me," she said. "You certainly hate me."

"No," I said while putting on my own clothes. "I just can't enter your body when it's breeding a child, and another man's child at that!"

12

I was very quiet when I came back from Shuzhou. I was too depressed to talk to anybody. My roommates tried to figure out what had happened to me, but they couldn't. I locked my lips and my tongue and refused to tell anybody.

Every Friday, it was painful when the others in my room went together to the dance while I had to find some excuse to avoid going with them. Sometimes, I had to leave the campus for a stroll in order to prove that I really had something to do.

Rambling about outside the campus was painful too. Every path held her track and every building reminded me of the time when we were together. I didn't know how could I free myself from the memory of her.

I cursed the unfairness of fate. Why was she another man's wife, not mine? Why had she been married before we found each other? If I had wanted to be a knight when I was a kid, now I wished I was the villain so that I could shamelessly take her away from her husband. Oh, the unfairness! We loved each other, but we couldn't be married! She loved me, but she had to stay with her husband!

Sometimes on campus, we would meet by chance. I couldn't help but notice that her inflated belly was always covered with books, a bag, or a satchel. She wore a jacket all the time, although it was already summer and the weather became warmer and warmer. I knew she was embarrassed to be noticed, since she was the only pregnant student on campus.

My roommates soon knew the truth because they had friends in the Chinese Department, and they knew she was married and now pregnant.

"I'm so sorry," Four-eyes said. "She shouldn't have let you sink into such a hopeless love for so long."

"I knew right away when I saw her," Wu said. "She's a married woman. Look at her body, she's not a girl anymore."

"Forget her," Fu said. "There are lots pretty girls in the world, and you certainly will find one."

"Yes. You'll have a degree; you are handsome; you will have a better choice."

"I don't care if I will have a better choice," I said. "I just think it's not fair."

"There *is* no fairness in the world," Four-eyes said. "You will drive yourself crazy if you want to find fairness."

"She can divorce," Andi said. "If she loves you."

"No," Wu said. "She has no chance."

"Then forget her," Lim said.

"Yes, forget her."

But I just couldn't forget her. Sometimes I hated myself because I couldn't stop loving her. She was my first girl, a girl who had shared everything with me.

She finally left school for home when the school year was over. She asked me to take her to the station so that we could say goodbye to each other one last time. It was in July. She was for the first time wearing a loose T-shirt. Because she had to carry two bags in her hands, she couldn't cover her full belly with other stuff in front of me.

"I don't know what you must think about me," she said and forced a smile. "But I still appreciate what did you give me in last three years."

I said nothing because I felt a lump in my throat. I took the book out of my bag and opened it with trembling hands. A withered, tiny flower lay silently between two pages. Tears like pearls dropped one by one; she picked the flower up carefully from the book.

"Take it," I said. "It's yours."

She sobbed and kissed it, then took her bags and walked toward the gate without looking back once.

"Fang-fang!" I cried. But I couldn't send out my voice, and I couldn't move either. I stood there like a blockhead, watching her disappear behind the door.

"No!" Suddenly, I jumped like a cornered beast and ran after her. But I was stopped by the watchers of the gate who asked me for the ticket.

"I don't have a ticket," I said. "I only want to say goodbye to my friend!"

"Then buy a platform ticket. One train ticket can buy two platform tickets," one of them told me.

But I didn't have a train ticket, I couldn't get the platform ticket. No matter how hard I tried, I still couldn't enter the gate. Oh, no! I paced up and down at my wit's end around that station, counting every second and minute. Finally when evening came, I knew I was lost. She had gone forever, no matter what could I do. It was all over now and my dream was finished. I was left, all alone!

Liu was shocked when he saw me standing in front of his house, ghastly pale. "What happened?" he drew me into his room and asked.

"No! Don't ask me anything right now."

"Oh, poor Li Ling," he sighed and held me into his arms. I started to cry. I cried loudly, cried my eyes out. I had never cried like that before; and I couldn't help it any. The tears ran down themselves.

Liu held me till I calmed down at last. "Poor Li Ling, I should have told you before."

"What?"

"Yes. She told me the first time she came here for dinner. She told me she had been married and had a child. I asked her if she wanted to keep the marriage, she said yes because she had owed her husband."

"Why didn't you tell me?"

"I promised her that I would keep the secret for her. And, I thought she would change her mind because she loved you." He sighed again and lowered his head. "I never expected it would come to such an ending."

"So I'm the only one who didn't know the truth," I said. I felt even more dejected when I left Liu for home. I was such a stupid fool who was kept in a drum for three years!

My parents finally knew when I told them Fang-fang was leaving. I didn't dare to tell them the truth because they could never accept the fact that she had been married before she became my girl-friend. It was a sin in China for a married woman like Fang-fang to fall in love with another man, although they knew her miserable life during the Revolution, and they might understand that it was a loveless marriage. I told them it was because of her mother's poor health that she had to leave for home and transfer to Anhui University afterward.

My parents felt sorry for me, since they knew how much I loved her. They also knew there was no possibility for me to go with her. I had no reason to transfer, and it wouldn't be allowed. "Maybe you can take a break and visit your grandparents this summer?" my father said.

My grandparents? Yes! I needed a break. I couldn't stay anymore in this place that had so much pain. I should leave for a while, maybe a couple of months, maybe several years, till I could face my fate again. I wrote to my grandparents and asked them for help, because I needed an invitation letter to apply for the passport.

In the letter, my grandma asked me if I would like to go abroad now. They still thought it was the best chance for me. "You could stop by when you leave for abroad and visit us," she said. I gave the letter to my parents.

"What do you think?" my father asked.

"Why not?" I said. Why not? If I had refused them because I had Fang-fang, now I had nothing to worry about. I would go; go anywhere but Anhui!

"Then tell them." My parents were all excited about the plan because they thought it would be wonderful for me. "You should see the world," my father said, "you should see how the other people live and work. You won't regret your decision, although you will miss your home, and we will miss you."

The last semester at school I was busy with writing letters, filling the forms, preparing for the English test, waiting for the results. I had applied to five schools, distributing over five states from east to west in the USA. The letters and application forms had helped to fill the hollow of my soul, and I was glad to find that at least I had something to keep myself busy so that I could forget the past.

Before the semester ended, I got answers. Three out of the five schools had accepted me. When I finally got what I wanted, I didn't feel happy but sad. Now I had to leave. Was it a good medicine to cure my pain? Could it let me forget? What was it all about?

My friends all wished me good luck; they wanted me to be the first PH.D holder of our school.

"I'll follow you next year," Four-eyes said. He was going to apply for graduate school. "I have to get the Bachelor's degree first so that I can apply for a T.A. or R.A. at the same time. My relatives can't support me as fully as your grandparents do."

"Good luck," I said. I knew it wasn't easy for a newcomer to get a T.A. or R.A. But he had to try it. It was the only way for him to go.

"Don't forget to visit us if you get the chance to come back to China," Wu said. "We will be very proud of your visiting, you know."

"I will. I hope by the time we are together, you have already gotten divorced and are living with a girl you love."

"I hope so. I will do my best to try."

"I hope you can help me to travel around the world someday when you become a rich man."

I laughed. "A millionaire. Only when I become a millionaire, you can have the opportunity. But since Andi wants me to become one, I would do my best."

"You will," Fu smiled and said. "You are smart; you are healthy. These two are decisive factors of success."

"Thank you."

"What about you, Lim?" Four-eyes asked Lim who was sitting beside me, smiling. "Don't you want to say something?"

"Oh," he blushed. "I only have a wish. I wish someday we can have a reunion not only in China, but also in America."

"Yes. That's the word!" Andi jumped and said.

Before I left, I went back to the rice center where I had spent more than five years, and said goodbye to my friends and my old colleagues. We shook hands, hugged, and wished every one good luck. They were all very busy and satisfied with what were they doing. The contract system seemed to work very well there.

Liu sent me to the airport with my parents. He was in love and he would marry Apple when they graduated.

"Good luck," he said quietly. "You will find your love in the strange land. Might be a western girl, believe it or not, with blue eyes and golden hair."

"Will I?" I smiled bitterly. "I don't think that I would ever fall in love again."

"You will, believe me."

"Take care," my mother said when they stopped in front of customs. "Write us as soon as you arrive."

"I will. Goodbye, Dad; Goodbye, Mom: Goodbye, Liu. I'll miss you!"

They waved farewells, and I rushed through the customs and fled. Only when I was alone behind the door, I cried out like a child. Oh, my dear country! My dear parents! My dear friends! Oh, my dear Fang-fang, my love! I loved you! Wherever I go, I will never stop loving you!

The plane roared and headed into the blue sky.

About the Author

Xiao-ming Chen, a native Chinese and current resident of Brookline, Massachusetts, was born in Shanghai, grew up in Hong Kong. She got her Bachelor's in Literature at Fudan University, Shanghai, and her Master's in Creative Writing at the University of New Mexico, Albuquerque. Although *The Tale of a Chinese* is her first book released in the United States, she has published five books in China including two novels and three translations. She has been an Assistant Professor at the Shanghai Institute of Foreign Languages and a Lecturer in Literature at Fudan University. Now she is working in Boston.